PLAY ALL THE GAMES,
SOLVE ALL THE PUZZLES—
READ ALL THE LEMONCELLOS!

MR. LEMONCELLO'S VERY FIRST GAME

ESCAPE FROM MR. LEMONCELLO'S LIBRARY

MR. LEMONCELLO'S LIBRARY OLYMPICS

MR. LEMONCELLO'S GREAT LIBRARY RACE

MR. LEMONCELLO'S ALL-STAR BREAKOUT GAME

MR. LEMONCELLO AND THE TITANIUM TICKET

MR. LEMONCELLO'S VERY FIRST GAME

CHRIS GRABENSTEIN

RANDOM HOUSE NEW YORK

Text copyright © 2022 by Chris Grabenstein
Jacket art copyright © 2022 by James Lancett

Random House and the colophon are registered trademarks of Penguin Random House LLC.

Photograph on p. v from the personal collection of Chris Grabenstein, used by permission.

Visit us on the Web! rhcbooks.com

Educators and librarians, for a variety of teaching tools, visit us at RHTeachersLibrarians.com

Library of Congress Cataloging-in-Publication Data
Name: Grabenstein, Chris, author.
Title: Mr. Lemoncello's very first game / Chris Grabenstein.
Description: First edition. | New York: Random House Children's Books, [2022]
Summary: Everybody starts somewhere, and once upon a time Luigi Lemoncello was a thirteen-year-old boy in a large family who dreamed of being a showman; he gets his first chance working for a famous barker at a summer carnival where a mysterious puzzle leads him and his friends on a treasure hunt.
Identifiers: LCCN 2021040047 | ISBN 978-0-593-48083-0 (trade) | ISBN 978-0-593-48084-7 (lib. bdg.) | ISBN 978-0-593-56745-6 (int'l) | ISBN 978-0-593-48086-1 (ebook)
Subjects: LCSH: Entertainers—Juvenile fiction. | Eccentrics and eccentricities—Juvenile fiction. | Treasure hunt (Game)—Juvenile fiction. | Carnivals—Juvenile fiction. | Friendship—Juvenile fiction. | CYAC: Entertainers—Fiction. | Eccentrics and eccentricities—Fiction. | Treasure hunt (Game)—Fiction. | Carnivals—Fiction. | Friendship—Fiction.
Classification: LCC PZ7.G7487 Mu 2021 | DDC 813.6 [Fic]—dc23

Printed in the United States of America
10 9 8 7 6 5 4 3 2 1
First Edition

FOR MY BROTHERS, DR. JEFF, DR. TOM, DR. BILL, AND LAWYER STEVE.
LUIGI LEMONCELLO WASN'T THE ONLY ONE WHO GREW UP WITH
AMAZINGLY TALENTED, SUPER-STRIVER SIBLINGS.

It was the summer that changed Luigi L. Lemoncello's life.

Which, of course, led to millions of other lives being changed. The events of that long-ago summer gave rise to families made closer by games played late into the night or on rainy vacation days. It also ushered in a magical factory, a spectacularly futuristic library, dazzling contests, an unquenchable quest for knowledge, stupendous surprises, and fantastic fun unlike any the world had ever seen or experienced.

But we're getting ahead of ourselves.

In 1968, Luigi had just turned thirteen. He was the sixth of the ten Lemoncello children. His older brothers and sisters were all super-serious, super-talented, straight-A students. Luigi, on the other hand, loved making up stories. He loved solving puzzles. And he really, really loved playing games.

Everyone said he was, well, different. Maybe even peculiar. Definitely odd.

On weekends, Luigi's father ran the projector at the Willoughby Bijou Theater on Main Street in Alexandriaville, Ohio. Whenever there was a Saturday matinee for kids, Mr. Lemoncello would sneak his children up to the projection booth with him.

It was the only way the whole family could afford to see movies.

For free.

The Lemoncello kids would take turns peering through the small window next to the clacking movie projector. They'd each watch for a few minutes and then tell their brothers and sisters what had happened.

"The millionaire was boxing with the bad guy," Luigi said after his turn at the window.

And then he added his own spin.

"That's when a kangaroo hopped into the ring!" he told his brothers and sisters.

"A kangaroo?" exclaimed the youngest Lemoncello, Sofia.

"Oh yes. And the kangaroo can really sing!"

Luigi's sixteen-year-old brother, Fabio, motioned for Luigi to step aside. "It's my turn. You're being goofy."

"No," said Sofia. "Let Luigi go again. He tells the best movies."

But Fabio wasn't about to give up his turn.

"Okay, now the guy who loves cars is singing a song about Detroit. . . ."

Luigi pressed his ear to the wall.

"DEE-TROIT! DEE-TROIT! DEEEEEEE-WOOOOO-WAAAA-TA-TA-TA-TA . . ."

The movie soundtrack warbled to a stop.

The Lemoncello kids, their eyes wide, swiveled to face their father.

"The projector's jammed," said Luigi's father with a frustrated sigh. "I told Mr. Willoughby we should replace this clunker. Stand back, everybody. I need to make a splice."

Mr. Lemoncello was very handy and could fix almost anything. He flicked up some light switches, shut down the clattering mechanical monster, and pulled both ends of the filmstrip out of its feed sprockets.

While his father wrestled with the two enormous film reels, Luigi heard the audience downstairs. They were chanting and stomping their feet.

"We want the movie!"

"We want the movie!"

Kids hurled boxes of popcorn. Sugar Babies and Sno-Caps bounced around the auditorium like spitballs.

"Go down and tell them about the singing kangaroo," Sofia urged Luigi.

"Huh?"

Luigi was used to telling his family stories. And his friends. Sometimes the kids at school.

But an auditorium filled with strangers?

"Go," said Sofia. "Hurry!"

"No!" hissed Luigi's oldest sister (and harshest critic), Mary. "Don't you dare embarrass us."

The crowd below was chanting louder. Their foot stomps became a thundering herd of cattle. Mr. Lemoncello was nimble and quick with his hands, but he needed more time.

"We want the movie!"

"We want the movie!"

Luigi looked over to Sofia.

She smiled. "You can do it!"

Luigi raced down the steep staircase from the projection booth, tore across the lobby, and slammed through the swinging double doors into the auditorium.

The theater was dim, but Luigi saw a soft circle of light pooling on the empty screen.

He ran down the center aisle.

Took a deep breath.

And stepped into the faint spotlight.

This was soooo different from telling his little sister a funny story. He could barely see kids in the seats, just their hazy silhouettes.

"Um, good afternoon, boys and girls," he began.

The kid shapes squirmed. They seemed annoyed or bored or both.

Luigi looked up to the projection booth. Sofia was in the window, smiling down at him.

He had to do . . . something.

"Uh, I bet you're all wondering what happens next!"

"Yeah!" yelled a voice from the darkness.

"Well, um, as they drive to Detroit, a big wind kicks up, and all of a sudden their car can fly—just like in *The Absent-Minded Professor*! They sail through the clouds and—"

THUNK! SPLAT!

A half-empty Pepsi cup smacked Luigi in the face. Sticky brown syrup dribbled down his nose.

"Sit down, weirdo," shouted a blond boy in the middle of the auditorium. He looked to be about fifteen.

The girl next to him squirmed in her seat. "Leave the kid alone, Chad."

Luigi figured he had two choices. He could run away, or he could stay and try to change the story he was suddenly starring in. Maybe even make it funny.

"Now, then," he said, comically wiping his face the way he'd seen the Three Stooges do after being clobbered by banana cream pies. "Where was I?"

"Blocking the screen!" shouted the guy named Chad. "Who do you think you are, anyhow?"

Good question, thought Luigi. Who was he?

"Uh, nobody, really."

"Well, do you know who *I* am?"

"The Mad Pepsi Bomber?"

The crowd laughed.

"No, weirdo. I'm Chad Chiltington. And my best friend

5

is Jimmy Willoughby. His old man owns this movie theater. How'd you sneak in here? You don't look like you could afford to buy a ticket. I'm going to report you to Mr. Willoughby!"

Uh-oh! thought Luigi. If Chad Chiltington did that, Luigi's father could lose his projectionist job.

"I'm sorry. I was just trying to—"

Suddenly, light flickered on the screen, warbly music slid up to speed, and the movie started. His dad had saved the day. The kids in the auditorium cheered. Chad Chiltington draped his arm over his girlfriend's shoulders. He also snagged her Pepsi cup, since he didn't have one anymore.

He had forgotten all about Luigi Lemoncello.

Well, Luigi sure hoped he had.

The Lemoncello family was so huge, they ate dinner every night the way some families do on Thanksgiving or Christmas.

With two tables.

Luigi's mother, father, and five older brothers and sisters sat at the big table. Luigi sat with his four youngest siblings at a fold-up card table. Stromboli, the cat, slept on the sideboard. Fusilli, the dog, sat patiently under the smaller "kids' table," because the younger Lemoncellos dropped the most food.

It had been a week since the incident at the movie theater.

Luckily, nothing bad had happened. Mr. Lemoncello still had his projectionist job. Luigi hadn't been barred for life from the movie theater. Nobody had thrown another half-empty cup at him. Even scowling Mary seemed to have forgotten it.

The Lemoncello family lived in a cramped apartment building at 21 Poplar Lane in what was called the Little Italy section of Alexandriaville. Most of their neighbors were Italian. Or Irish. Or Polish. The Italians had arrived first, so the crowded cluster of four-story brownstone buildings was named after them.

"Here you go, guys," said Luigi, pulling three hand-drawn cards out of an envelope. He placed them side by side on the kids' table. "It's a new game. I just invented it."

"What is it?" asked Alberto, who was eight.

"A secret code!" said Luigi.

"Neat," said ten-year-old Arianna.

"Cool," said Massimo, who was the second youngest, at six.

The first card showed a dog. The second, an orange. A goat was on the third. Luigi tapped the three cards, one at a time.

"In this game, you have to figure out what I'm spelling by using the first letters of the pictures. For instance, this is how you'd spell 'dog.' *D-O-G*."

Five-year-old Sofia had a puzzled expression on her face.

"Why do you need all those cards to spell 'dog'?" she asked. "The first one has a dog on it."

The big table erupted with laughter. Luigi's older brothers and sisters were all watching.

"Always with the games," said the oldest, eighteen-year-old Tomasso.

"You should spend more time studying!" said Mary, who was the next oldest, at seventeen. "Make something out of yourself. Quit being such an oddball."

Luigi had heard this before. Many, many times. Most of his brothers and sisters already knew what they wanted to do when they grew up. Fabio was going to be a lawyer. His teachers had been telling him since kindergarten that he'd make a good one.

Francesca, on the other hand, would become a doctor. A brain surgeon. She was only fifteen but had already figured out her whole life.

"What're you going to do, Luigi?" asked Lucrezia, who was only one year older than Luigi. "Waste your time playing games?"

"Break another window?" said Tomasso, shaking his head.

"Maybe shatter some more mirrors?" added Mary.

Ugh, thought Luigi. *Nobody's ever going to forget that.*

Last winter, during a blizzard, when everyone had been stuck inside the cramped apartment, Luigi had had an idea for a game.

It included a golf ball.

And a slingshot.

When it was Alberto's turn, he went for a toilet-bowl plunk-and-plop.

Unfortunately, Alberto ricocheted his shot off the medicine cabinet (shattering the mirror) and out the bathroom window (shattering *that* glass too).

Mr. Lemoncello, who was extremely clever, tacked up an old woolen blanket and a sheet of cardboard to block out the gusting winter wind. He also worked out a payment plan with the landlord to have the window and the medicine-cabinet mirror replaced.

And even though it had been Alberto who actually broke the mirror and window, everyone knew the truth.

It was all Luigi's fault.

He picked up his handmade game cards and slid them back into the envelope.

Soon steaming bowls of food, with wheels on their bottoms, rolled around the table on the train-track device Mr. Lemoncello had engineered to make serving dinner to twelve hungry people faster. Everyone forgot about Luigi and his First Letters game.

Everybody except Luigi.

"Did you hear?" said Lucrezia. "The Poliseis are going to Florida for vacation!"

"We should go to Florida!" grumbled Arianna.

"Your father would need to *get* a vacation first," said Mrs. Lemoncello. "And Mr. Willoughby doesn't believe in them. Neither does the Belkin Bicycle Factory."

Mr. Lemoncello glanced at his watch. He had three different jobs. The seven-to-three shift at the bicycle factory. Night janitor at the big department store downtown. And weekend work at the movie theater. None of them gave him a vacation or paid enough for a trip to Florida.

Luigi sometimes felt it was his fault that his dad had to work so hard. After all, he was the one always breaking things that cost money to replace. He was the one who wasn't going to grow up to be a fancy doctor or lawyer. Maybe Luigi needed to get his head out of the clouds.

"There's a reason most people only dream at night," Mary often reminded him. "Bad things happen when you do it during the day!"

When he finished changing his clothes after church the next day, Luigi bolted out the back door of his apartment building to meet his two best friends.

Bruno Depinna and Chester Raymo were both thirteen, like Luigi. They were waiting for him in the crackled asphalt alleyway that was their hangout.

Luigi had a mop of curly black hair, black eyes, and what some people called olive skin, even though Luigi had never thought he looked all that green.

Bruno was a beefy kid with a buzz cut and the same olive complexion as Luigi's. But that was where the similarities ended. Luigi felt everything with his heart first. Bruno went with his gut—or sometimes his fists.

Chester was the brains of the group. He had brown hair and perpetually puckered lips, as if he were waiting for a fish to kiss him. Chester loved tearing apart gadgets and gizmos so he could dream up his own. In that way, he was a lot like Luigi's dad.

Up on the fourth floor, piano music wafted out an open window. Luigi's little sister Arianna was practicing again.

"Is that Beethoven's 'Für Elise'?" asked Chester.

"Yeah," said Luigi. "Arianna's very talented. Her piano teacher says everyone has a gift, and Arianna's is music."

"I could never play the piano," said Bruno. "On account of my hands. They're the size of canned hams."

"Hey," said Luigi, "either of you guys ever heard of Chad Chiltington?"

"Uh, yeah," said Bruno. "His old man runs the bank. Wouldn't give my pops a loan when he wanted to open up a second butcher shop. The rich are the only ones who ever get richer. The rest of us? Forget about it."

"Actually," said Chester, "I think, if we use our heads and work hard, we can all become millionaires."

"Yeah, right," said Bruno. "Like that's ever going to happen."

"Hey," said Luigi, "we might even become bajillionaires!"

Another window creaked open on the fourth floor. The boys looked up to see Luigi's father. He jabbed two fingers into the corners of his mouth and shrieked out an ear-piercing whistle.

"Dinnertime! Tomasso, Mary, Fabio, Francesca . . . all of you. Come home! Dinnertime."

Bruno chuckled and shook his head. "Does your father even know all your names?"

"Someday, I guarantee he's going to know mine," Luigi comically proclaimed before heading inside for the family's Sunday midday meal. "I am going to be the most famous Lemoncello of them all. Who knows? I might even be the world's first bajillionaire!"

As June became July, Luigi, Chester, and Bruno grew restless.

There were only so many sticks they could throw for Fusilli to chase, even if Luigi made up exciting stories that turned those sticks into James Bond spy gear.

"You've got what they call a hyperactive imagination," Bruno told Luigi. "It's like a factory, cranking out all sorts of wacky ideas."

"But I'm bored," said Chester, fitting a chunk of asphalt back into its hole in the pavement, as if he were working a jigsaw puzzle.

"Because you miss math class," joked Bruno.

"Hang on," said Luigi. "I've got just the thing."

"What is it?" asked Bruno. "An old homework assignment? Fractions?"

"Nope. A game I've been working on."

"Ah, why do you always want to make a game?"

Luigi shrugged. "I guess so guys like us won't be bored out of our gourds every July."

He raced back into the apartment building and headed up the stairs to the fourth floor.

Why *did* he want to make a game?

Of course, he loved *playing* games. Games were fun and challenging and exciting. They also had rules that couldn't be broken. Games were fair. Life sometimes wasn't.

Luigi raised his mattress and slid out the manila envelope filled with clue cards for what he was still calling his First Letters game. He'd had a new idea about the secret codes. A way to turn the game into a competition to make it more fun. He grabbed three pencils and a few pieces of scrap paper off the homework desk he shared with his brothers.

"Okay," he told his friends when he was back in the alley. "I'm going to pick seven random cards and make the best, longest word I can come up with out of those letters."

He shook out the A–Z picture cards upside down on top of a garbage can's lid in the alleyway. He turned over seven of them.

"Apple equals *A*?" said Chester.

"Is this game for kindergartners?" asked Bruno.

Luigi ignored them as he studied the *A, C, E, O, R, D,* and *F* cards.

"The cat is C," mumbled Bruno. "Oh yeah. Super exciting."

"This is where things get interesting," said Luigi. "I'm going to think of a word that uses some or all of these letters only once. I'll write that word on this slip of paper. You guys will each study the same letters and then write down one word on your slips of paper. If you guess my word, you get points."

"How many?" asked Chester.

Luigi shrugged. "I dunno. Ten?"

Bruno nodded. "Ten sounds good."

"If you guys don't guess my word," Luigi continued, "I score the ten points."

"How many points do we need to win?" asked Chester.

Luigi thought about that. "A hundred!"

Bruno nodded again. "That's what I would've said. A hundred. Maybe fifty if we were in a hurry."

Luigi looked at the cards again:

A, C, E, O, R, D, F

He could make *CAR*. Or *FAR*. Even *FACE*.

But then he got a better idea. A word that might baffle his opponents. He wrote it down on a slip of paper and folded it in half.

"Okay. Go. What word do you think I made up?"

"This is like the Jumble puzzle in the funny pages," said Bruno. He wrote down his guess and doubled over the paper four times to make sure Chester couldn't see his answer.

Luigi waited for Chester to write down a word too.

"Done!" Chester announced.

"What've you got?" Luigi asked him.

"'Road,'" said Chester. "*R-O-A-D*!"

"Nope," said Luigi.

"'Face,'" guessed Bruno. "*F-A-C-E*."

"*SCRONK!*" said Luigi. "That answer is also incorrect." He unfolded his slip of paper. "'Ford.' *F-O-R-D*."

"That's a proper name!" said Chester. "You can't use proper names."

Luigi gave him a look. "Um, I don't remember that being in the rules. . . ."

"Well," said Chester, "it should've been. It's a rule in Scrabble."

"'Ford' also means to cross a river. You know"—Luigi started warbling—"'climb every mountain . . . ford every stream . . .'"

"That's only in Norway," Bruno protested. "They taught us about that in geography last year."

Luigi laughed. "Those are fjords. Not fords. Fjords."

The three friends were laughing and cracking each other up, ready to play the next round. Fusilli wagged his tail. He wanted the game to keep going too. Luigi flipped over the cards they'd just played and slid the pile around on the garbage can lid.

"You could also use these cards to communicate in

18

code," he said. "If you wanted to say, 'Meet me after school,' the secret code would be monkey, elephant, elephant—"

Luigi froze mid-phrase.

Because two blond boys in plaid shorts had just strolled into the alley.

And one was the boy from the movie theater.

"See, Chad?" said the other blond boy. "This is where all the riffraff live."

The two boys were fifteenish but looked like they could already belong to a college fraternity. Fusilli didn't like either of them. He dropped down to the ground and growled.

Chad pointed a finger at Luigi. "This is the wacko who snuck into your father's movie theater."

When Chad said that, Luigi realized something that made his stomach clench: the other boy was James Willoughby. His father, who was also named James Willoughby, owned the movie theater *and* the department store where Luigi's father swept the floors and cleaned the toilets.

"Never come back to my family's movie theater," Willoughby said to Luigi. "We don't really want your type in our auditorium."

Bruno bristled. "Oh yeah? And what type is that?"

"Troublemakers," said Willoughby.

"You boys should stay where you belong," added Chiltington.

"Actually," said Chester, "there are no laws against free ingress—"

"Thanks to you, Jenny Grabowski won't go out with me again!" Chiltington shouted at Luigi.

"Sorry," said Luigi. "Who's Jenny Grabowski?"

"The girl I took to the movies. She thought I was being mean when I told you to shut up and sit down."

Bruno arched an eyebrow. "Were you screaming then like you're screaming now? Because, I gotta tell you, pal, it is pretty obnoxious."

"Anybody ever tell you you've got a smart mouth?"

"Nah," said Bruno. "Usually, they're more impressed by my smart clothes. I'm what they call a snappy dresser."

"I oughta pound you, punk."

Bruno smiled and took a step forward. "No. You seriously do not want to do that. Trust me. This is *my* neighborhood. Whole lot of 'riffraff' and 'troublemakers' live round here."

Fear flashed across Chiltington's eyes. He looked up and down the alley. Like he expected an angry gang or maybe Bruno's big brothers to leap out of the shadows.

"We should get out of here, Chad," whispered Jimmy. "Dad says to be careful in this neighborhood."

"So why does he own all the buildings over here?" snarled Chiltington.

"To make money!"

Luigi's stomach did another somersault.

Mr. Willoughby owned the Lemoncellos' home? He was their landlord?

"Come on, Chad," said Jimmy. "This alley gives me the creeps."

"Hang on." Chiltington grabbed Luigi's playing cards off the garbage-can lid.

"You draw these pictures?" he sneered. "The widdle cat and widdle doggy?"

"Yeah."

Chiltington tore the thin cardboard apart and tossed the pieces up into the air like confetti.

"We're not playing games, boys," said Chiltington. "Stay away from the Willoughby movie theater. Or this . . ."

He tossed up another clump of shredded cards.

". . . will be you."

They strolled away, laughing.

"Sorry," Bruno said to Luigi. "They ripped up your game."

Luigi shrugged it off.

"It's okay. I have another set of cards upstairs. Besides, it might've been my first idea for a game, but to be honest, it might've also been my worst." He grinned at his friends. "The next one I come up with? Oh, it will be ten times better, or my name isn't Luigi L. Lemoncello!"

"Hey, did you hear?" said Chester. "They've got the new Hardy Boys mystery at the library."

"No, Chester," said Bruno. "I did not hear that. Then again, I'm not a nerd like some people I know."

The three friends were walking down Market Street, heading toward the Alexandriaville Public Library. Chester was the biggest bookworm in the bunch, but Luigi and Bruno liked the library too. That's where Luigi could think about and tinker with his game ideas, something that was hard to do in his crowded home. He also loved the magazines that had puzzles and games in them.

Bruno liked the library because it was air-conditioned. And because it had sports magazines.

"Thanks for hanging with me, you guys," said Chester.

"Hey, what choice do we have?" asked Bruno.

"None," said Luigi. "We are, after all, the three musketeers!"

"'Fun for all and all for fun'?" said Bruno, repeating a line from the candy bar commercials.

"Bruno," said Chester, "you do realize that before it was a candy bar, *The Three Musketeers* was a book."

"So you keep telling me. But when, exactly, did the author decide to turn his book into a delicious snack?"

Luigi laughed. Chester shook his head.

The Alexandriaville Public Library was two blocks west of Main Street. A squat brick building, it was only two windows and a doorway wide.

It did have a pair of what Mrs. Tobin, the librarian, called classical Doric columns on either side of its short front porch. Mrs. Tobin was always trying to teach them stuff like classical architecture. Some of it stuck. Mostly with Chester.

But Luigi did know that the Alexandriaville Public Library was a Carnegie library, built with money donated by the millionaire tycoon Andrew Carnegie. According to Mrs. Tobin, Carnegie had built 1,689 public libraries in the United States. Luigi thought it might be cool to do something like that someday. But first he'd have to become a tycoon.

He saw Mrs. Tobin unlocking the front door.

"Good morning, bookworms!" she called out.

"Good morning, Mrs. Tobin!" Chester and Luigi hollered back.

Bruno grunted a little and waved.

Fusilli would wait outside while the three friends were in the library. He usually took a nap in the shade of a leafy oak tree in the middle of the library's tidy lawn.

The Alexandriaville Public Library had a collection of board games. Luigi would sometimes take two or three off the shelves, mix up the playing pieces, the cards, and the dice, and then make up his own rules to create a brand-new game.

"We have some new books, boys," Mrs. Tobin announced as she switched on the lights. She was dressed, as usual, in a bell-shaped dress with a wide white collar. She also wore a beaded necklace and cat-eye glasses.

"Since you all liked *The Book of Three* so much, I made sure we had extra copies of Lloyd Alexander's new one: *The High King*. Oh, Luigi—I also have the science book your sister Francesca put on hold."

"Thanks," said Luigi.

Yes, his sister, the one who was only two years older than him, was still studying, even though school was out. Meanwhile, Luigi was wasting his summer playing games.

He and his friends hadn't been at the library long when nine-year-old Vinny Ciccarelli arrived. Vinny smiled and waved at Luigi, but, like always, he didn't say anything other than a mumbled "Hi."

"Vincent Ciccarelli is painfully shy," Mrs. Tobin had once told Luigi. "I think it's why he likes the library so much. *Everybody* is quiet here."

Luigi went out of his way to talk to Vinny whenever he saw the boy sitting quietly in a library chair, his feet too short to reach the floor.

"Hey, did you know there's going to be an Olympics this year?" he whispered when he noticed Vinny leafing through a copy of *Sports Illustrated*.

Vinny shook his head.

"I think there should be a *library* Olympics," Luigi went on. "There could be all sorts of competitions. Speed reading. Book balancing. Maybe even library-cart races."

Vinny smiled. "You're wacky, Luigi Lemoncello," he said before going back to his magazine.

True, thought Luigi. *But I also got you to say four whole words!*

Luigi decided to go home with the May edition of a magazine that had Hidden Pictures and Mind Stretcher games in it. Chester checked out a book called *From the Mixed-Up Files of Mrs. Basil E. Frankweiler.* Bruno enjoyed the air-conditioning.

"Will you boys be attending the summer carnival?" Mrs. Tobin asked as she stamped the due dates on their checkout cards. "Opening day is this Saturday. Should be exciting!"

Outside, Fusilli started barking.

"He never barks like that," said Chester.

"Unless there's trouble," added Luigi.

There was.

The front doors swung open.

And Chad Chiltington stepped into the library.

"I can't believe they allow riffraff such as you three to—"

Luigi stepped aside so Chad could see that Mrs. Tobin was seated right there at her desk, casually thumping a date stamper on its spongy ink pad.

"May I help you, young man?" asked Mrs. Tobin. Apparently, Chad Chiltington had never visited the Alexandriaville Public Library before. Otherwise Mrs. Tobin would've known his name.

"Oh, good morning. I take it you're the librarian?"

"That's right."

"My, that necklace certainly is fetching. Are those real pearls?"

Mrs. Tobin grinned. "Hardly."

"Mrs. Tobin?" A large woman in stockings that made swishing noises whenever she moved her legs bustled into the library lobby.

"Good morning, Mrs. Chiltington. How may I help you?"

"By doing something about the mangy stray roaming about outside."

"That's Fusilli," explained Luigi. "He's harmless."

"Oh, really? The nasty beast barked at me. I've repeatedly told Mayor Hannigan that this city needs to hire a dogcatcher. I'll have to remind him again."

While she fussed and fumed about Fusilli, Mrs. Chiltington also sized up Luigi, Bruno, and Chester. From the look on her face, she didn't like what she saw.

"Whose children are these?" she inquired.

"Their parents'," replied Mrs. Tobin cheerfully.

That made Luigi smile.

Mrs. Chiltington frowned. "And they're checking out library books?"

"Of course. They're some of my biggest readers."

Now all three boys held their heads a little higher.

"But, honestly, Gail—do you really want to let just anybody, no matter how . . . *questionable* borrow the books our hard-earned tax dollars have paid for?"

Mrs. Tobin sat up straighter in her chair. "Of course I do. Knowledge not shared remains unknown. A public library's mission is to democratize information. To make it available to all who walk through our doors seeking it."

Mrs. Chiltington's whole face puckered up like she'd just sucked a dozen lemons. "I see."

"They also have good air-conditioning," cracked Bruno.

Mrs. Chiltington harrumphed. "Come along, Chadwick. Fortunately, we don't need a *public* library. We have plenty of books at home."

Mrs. Chiltington flounced out the door.

Chad flounced out behind her.

Fusilli started barking again.

He didn't like the Chiltingtons.

Dogs are very good judges of people.

"So it's almost eleven-thirty," said Luigi as he and his friends hurried up Poplar Lane, heading for home. "*Concentration* will be coming on! Can we watch it at your house, Bruno?"

"I guess we better if we want to hear it," said Bruno, digging in his jeans for his door keys.

"Yeah," said Chester. "Nothing personal, Luigi, but your house is noy-zee!"

"I know," said Luigi. "It's why I like the library so much."

Fusilli scampered home. He was a very self-reliant dog. Luigi and his friends hurried up to the Depinnas' apartment on the second floor. Mrs. Depinna offered them all some Kool-Aid. It was cherry, cold, and good.

Concentration was Luigi's favorite TV show because it was two games in one: a memory match and a rebus puzzle. First you had to clear the board by matching pairs of prizes hidden behind squares numbered 1 to 30. The contestants took home things like end-table lamps, hair dryers, and chafing dishes. Luigi had no idea what a chafing dish was.

As the matches were removed from the board, more and more of the rebus puzzle behind them was revealed.

"How come they call it a rebus puzzle?" asked Bruno.

"Because 'a puzzle that combines pictures and letters to spell out words and phrases' is too long," said Luigi.

The boys settled in and studied the puzzle being revealed, two blocks at a time. Luigi figured out the solution pretty quickly, but he didn't blurt it out—his friends were still playing.

Even after the whole puzzle was revealed, the TV guessers couldn't figure it out.

Neither could Bruno or Chester.

So Luigi went ahead and solved it out loud. "'Eye donut bell leaf waaa ice *E*.'"

"What?" said Bruno. "That makes absolutely no sense!"

Luigi smiled. "True. How about 'I do not believe what I see'?"

Two seconds later a buzzer *SCRONK*ed, and the game-show host gave his baffled contestants the same answer.

Luigi had nailed it! His friends whistled and clapped him on the back.

"I do not believe what *I* see," said Bruno. "You solving that messed-up mishmash."

"Too bad you can't make a living playing games and solving puzzles," said Chester.

"Yeah," said Bruno. "That'd show Mary you're not a goofball."

"Well, you are," said Chester. "But you're other stuff too."

Luigi laughed. On TV, the host said goodbye. That meant it was noon.

"I have to head home," said Luigi. "Mom likes it when we're all together for lunch. See you guys later."

"Not if we see you first!" joked Bruno.

Luigi scampered down the stairwell and hit the sidewalk. If he hurried, he'd be home before his mom magically turned a loaf of Wonder Bread into ten peanut butter and jelly sandwiches.

But Luigi saw something that made him freeze in his tracks.

His father. Slowly climbing the stoop of their apartment building, one heavy step at a time. His shoulders were slumped.

This was scary.

Luigi's father never came home from the bicycle factory for lunch.

Never.

Finally, after staring at the front door for what seemed like hours, Luigi's father pulled it open and heaved a sorrowful sigh.

He stepped into the foyer and began the four-story climb to the top floor.

Luigi, treading as lightly as he could, followed his father, making sure he was always at least one flight behind him and hidden from sight.

He heard his father open the front door to their apartment.

"Lucrezia?" said Luigi's father. "Please fetch Momma."

Luigi backed up against the stairwell wall.

"Angelo?" he heard his mother say as she came out to the landing. "What's wrong?"

"Close the door. I don't want the children to hear this."

The door creaked shut.

"So?" asked Luigi's mother. "What is it?"

"The factory laid me off."

Luigi's mother gasped.

"They're not selling enough bicycles," his father explained. "Nobody wants the kind we make anymore. But don't worry. I'll find a new job."

"I'll tighten the budget," said Luigi's mother.

"And I'll still be the janitor for Mr. Willoughby's department store. Plus, I have my weekend work at his movie theater. . . ."

Luigi's heart sank. If Mr. Willoughby found out about the stunt Luigi had pulled at the movie theater . . .

"Speaking of Mr. Willoughby," he heard his mother say, "he sent us another letter today. About the money we owe for the repairs. He's going to start charging interest."

"Everything is going to be okay," said Mr. Lemoncello, his voice brightening. "You'll see. I'll have more time for tinkering with my own inventions."

Luigi's father was putting on a brave face, but Luigi knew the truth. If you needed three jobs to support your family, you weren't all of a sudden okay with just two.

There were too many mouths to feed. Too many bills to pay. Too many shoes to buy.

Too many broken windows and bathroom mirrors.

"I really shouldn't go this year," Luigi told Bruno and Chester as they hiked across town on their way to Alexandriaville's annual summer carnival on opening night. "I don't have any money."

"That's okay," said Chester. "You can still go. It's a free country, after all."

"Then how come everything costs so much?" cracked Bruno.

"How about I spot you guys twenty-five cents each?" said Chester, jingling the change in his pocket. "I've been saving up. Plus, my mom and dad gave me my allowance a day early!"

Bruno stuck out his hand. Chester gave him a quarter. "Thanks. I'm gonna use this to buy a funnel cake. You two can watch me eat it."

"If I had twenty-five cents, I'd play a game," said Luigi.

"I said I'd give you a quarter," said Chester, reaching back into his pocket. Luigi waved him off.

"That's okay. I don't need to play tonight."

"Wise move," said Bruno. "Carnival games are a rip-off. The guys running the booths? They're all con artists and crooks."

As they walked closer to the fairgrounds on the edge of town, where the carnival was set up, Luigi could smell those deep-fried funnel cakes Bruno was so eager to eat.

The summer carnival, with its hastily erected Ferris wheel, Tilt-A-Whirl, and carousel, was only in Alexandriaville for ten days—that Saturday through the following Monday. There was a brightly lit midway filled with game booths and striped tents and food wagons and calliope music and squeals of laughter.

Chester pointed. "Check it out!"

"What?" said Bruno.

"That booth over there. The one with all the balloons and stuffed animals."

"So?" said Bruno. "It's just a balloon-pop game."

"Nuh-uh," said Chester. "Wait for it."

The booth, which was really a long trailer with a hitch so it could be towed to the next town on the carnival circuit, had chaser lights mounted up top. When they stopped blinking and swirling, they spelled out the name of the game.

BALLOON-CENTRATION

"Balloon-centration?" said Luigi.

"Uh-oh," said Bruno. "Sounds a lot like someone's favorite TV game show."

The three friends hurried toward the brightly lit booth. They could hear a carnival barker's voice calling out, "Step right up. Only five cents per throw!"

Every time a balloon popped, it revealed another part of a hidden picture puzzle.

"It *is* the same as *Concentration*," said Luigi.

"And the big prizes are pretty cool," said Chester.

Luigi looked at some of the items lined up on the prize shelves. Sure, there were a lot of stuffed animals, but he also spotted a toaster, a coffee percolator, and, yes, a chafing dish.

Luigi's mind started spinning. He was pretty good at solving the game show's puzzles on TV. What if he could win one of the big prizes in the booth, like the toaster, and sell it? He could help his mom and dad pay the bills this month. Ha! What would Mary say about that?

"You should play, Luigi," said Bruno.

"It only costs a nickel a dart," said Chester.

"You can use the quarter Chester loaned me," added Bruno.

Luigi shook his head. "That's your funnel-cake money."

Bruno shrugged and handed Luigi the coin Chester had given him. "I ate a big dinner."

"Here," said Chester, forcing a second quarter into Luigi's palm. "Take this, too. Now you've got enough for ten darts. Win my mom a teddy bear. I never could."

"I can't take your money, guys," Luigi protested.

"You'd better," said Bruno, raising his fist playfully.

"Okay, okay. I'll pay you back if I don't win."

"But you *are* going to win," said Bruno. "Balloon-centration? Come on, Luigi. This game has your name written all over it!"

Rolling the two quarters around in his hand, Luigi hurried toward the booth and found a spot near the next shooter.

Chester and Bruno crowded in behind him.

They watched a high school boy warm up his arm for a dart toss.

"Stand back, kid," he said to Luigi. "You're crowdin' me."

"Sorry." Luigi inched backward.

"Win me the purple bunny, Jack!" said his girlfriend.

"You got it, babe."

Jack tossed a dart with a great deal of oomph. It missed every single balloon on the board.

"Oh dear," said the barker. "I believe you were aiming at a target somewhere in Pennsylvania. This, as I recall, is Ohio."

Luigi had to laugh. Especially when he zeroed in on the carnival man's very unusual hat. It looked like a bunch of bananas in a bowl. Like something the Chiquita banana lady would wear.

And people say I'm strange, Luigi thought with a grin.

"Ready for your next throw?" the barker asked Jack. "Maybe this time you'll pop a balloon up in Michigan!"

The crowd laughed.

Jack plunked thirty cents down on the counter.

The man in the banana hat handed him six darts.

Jack threw them fast—*FLICK-FLICK-FLICK-FLICK-FLICK-FLICK.* A half-dozen balloons popped. The man behind the counter squeezed one of the rubber bananas in his hat.

SQUONK!

It burp-squeaked like one of Fusilli's dog toys.

The first pieces of the puzzle were revealed.

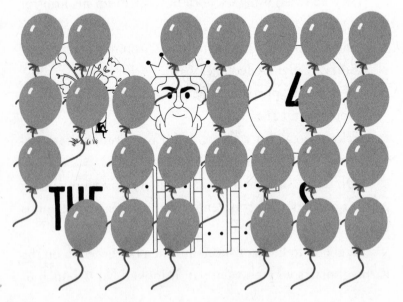

The barker was impressed. "Well done, Jack, if I may call you that, because from what I've heard, that is indeed your name."

"It is," said Jack.

"We all call him that," added his girlfriend.

"Well, that certainly makes things easier. Jack, you may call me Professor Marvelmous, for I am both marvelous and famous." The man tipped his banana hat. He had wispy white hair, bushy eyebrows, a curled mustache, chubby chipmunk cheeks, and elfin eyes. His coat was made of shiny satin with sparkly sequined lapels. None of the other booth operators were as outlandishly costumed as the balloon-pop man who called himself Professor Marvelmous. And, in Luigi's opinion, none of them were half as entertaining, either.

"You're famous?" asked the high school girl.

"Oh yes," replied the professor. "Why, I have popped balloons with kings, queens, potentates, and high, exalted grand pooh-bahs—which, of course, should never be confused with high, exalted grand Pooh Bears."

"You're weird, man," said Jack.

"Thank you for that compliment, my fine muscle-flexing fellow. Now then, Jack-a-roo, can you solve the hidden puzzle? If so, you could win a plush and pulchritudinous purple bunny!"

"That's the one I want, Jack," said the girl.

Jack plunked down sixty cents.

"Oooh," said Professor Marvelmous. "If I'm doing my

43

math correctly in my head—which, I must say, is much tidier than doing my math on paper, what with all those rubber eraser flecks—you would like to purchase a dozen more dart tosses."

"That's right, old man."

"Very well. A bold and audacious move." Professor Marvelmous turned to the girl. "Ma'am? You have a boldacious beau! Play on, boldacious Jack! Play on!"

Luigi was enjoying the professor's banter and antics so much, he nearly forgot about the game and the puzzle. Although, glancing at what had been revealed, he had a pretty good idea what the solution was.

Jack tossed a dozen darts. Six popped balloons. Six missed.

More of the puzzle was revealed.

Professor Marvelmous gave his banana hat another hearty honk.

SQUONK!

Luigi focused on the puzzle. Oh yeah. He definitely knew the answer.

"Jack?" said the professor. "For all the money—I mean, all the bunny—would you like to solve the puzzle?"

"Yeah," said Jack. "I'd *like* to. But I have no idea what it says."

"So keep throwing darts!" urged his girlfriend.

"No way, Diane. I'm not giving this geezer any more of my money. This game is a swindle. Nobody could solve that puzzle."

Professor Marvelmous gasped and, with a hand to his heart, bristled at the suggestion. "A swindle? I assure you, good sir, this puzzle is certainly solvable if not soluble."

Jack looked confused.

"'Soluble' means 'able to be dissolved,'" said Chester. "Like Kool-Aid is soluble in water."

"And, like, who cares, dweeb?" said Jack.

"Besides me?" said Chester. "Probably nobody."

Bruno laughed.

"What are *you* laughing at?" the high schooler said, his voice suddenly threatening.

As Bruno's face flushed red, Luigi stepped forward.

"He's laughing at how easy the puzzle is," he said.

"Easy?" said Jack. "Who are you three little punks, anyhow?"

"I, good sir, am Luigi L. Lemoncello," he said with a showy swirl of his hand, mimicking Professor Marvelmous. "In my humble opinion, this puzzle is simple and easy. Why, I daresay it's simpleasy!"

When Luigi said that, Professor Marvelmous arched a bushy eyebrow and smiled so broadly that his cheeks dimpled.

"Very well, Luigi L. Lemoncello. If it is, as you say, simpleasy, I challenge *you* to solve it!"

"So it's okay if I help Jack?" Luigi asked. "Because I wouldn't have a clue as to what the puzzle said if, you know, Jack here hadn't cleared the way for me."

Luigi was laying it on pretty thick. He didn't want the hulking high schooler mad at him, Bruno, or Chester.

"Of course you can help," said Professor Marvelmous. "'Fun for all and all for fun' is what I say."

Luigi, Bruno, and Chester looked at each other. The professor knew their rallying cry!

"Of course," he continued, "that's also what they say in a Three Musketeers candy bar commercial. Proceed, Luigi L. Lemoncello. Proceed."

Luigi took a deep breath and studied the puzzle one last time. He was pretty sure he knew the answer, but this was different from shouting it out at Bruno's TV. He tried to ignore the crowd waiting to take a turn. And

Jack, who was glaring at him like he didn't have a chance. But this *was* a game. Everyone who played had a chance to win!

"Okay, the first image is a kid on a swing. Next, we have a king, the number four, the word 'the,' a fence, and the letter *S*. Put it all together and you get 'Swing king four the fence *S*, or 'Swinging for the fences'!"

"Oh yeah," said Bruno. "Luigi just knocked it out of the park!"

Professor Marvelmous opened his eyes so wide they could've been hard-boiled eggs. Then he reached up and, squeezing several different bananas on his hat, burp-squeaked a triumphant fanfare.

SQUONK-SQUONK,SQUONKITY-SQUAAAAACK!

"Well done!" He pulled the stuffed bunny off its peg and handed it to the girl. "Here you are, my dear."

The happy couple strolled away.

Professor Marvelmous stomped a foot pump and quickly inflated a dozen new balloons. He placed them in the empty spots on the board, then cranked a scroll that moved a new hidden puzzle into place behind the wall of wobbly rubber.

"Now then, young man, are you ready to play on your own?"

Luigi felt a strange tingling sensation. There was something about Professor Marvelmous. Something . . . electric! Everything about this place—the flashing lights, the fluffy and shiny prizes, the thrill of victory—felt almost magical. Luigi carefully placed one of his two quarters on the counter.

"I'll start with five darts."

Professor Marvelmous swiped the quarter away with a quick flick of his finger. Luigi heard it plink into a money tray.

"Here you are, good sir. Your quiver of arrows."

Luigi was so nervous, his first four tosses missed the balloons and jabbed several of the stuffed animals framing the puzzle board. What a waste!

Luigi took a deep breath and flung his final dart.

POP!

One balloon burst to reveal the tiniest piece of the new puzzle.

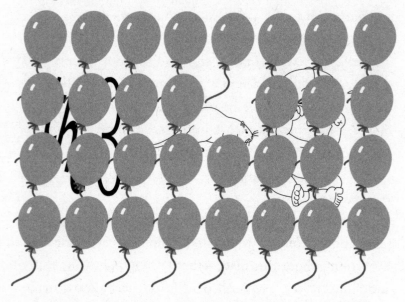

Luigi plunked down his second quarter.

"That's the quarter I gave you," said Bruno. "It'll be luckier."

"Hey," said Chester, "I gave *you* the quarter you gave to Luigi."

"True. But it picked up some extra luck while I was holding it."

Luigi threw five more darts.

Only one balloon popped.

The crowd laughed.

"Great aim, kid," teased a stranger, earning Luigi even more mean laughs. It reminded him of when his older brothers and sisters had mocked his silly First Letters game.

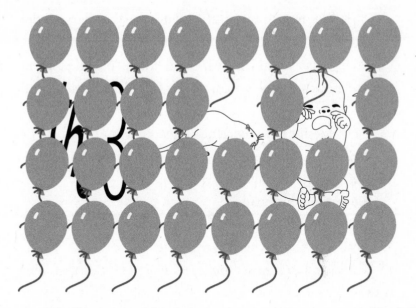

"Professor?" said Luigi.

"Yes?"

"I could solve the puzzle if . . ."

"If what?"

"If I could pop a few more balloons."

"Ah, you're wasting everybody's time, kid," groused a man.

Professor Marvelmous ignored the heckler and kept his twinkling eyes locked on Luigi.

"The puzzle always gets easier the more of it that you see."

Luigi stood up straight. "I can solve it in two more balloon pops."

The crowd oohed.

"That's impossible," shouted a woman.

"Two darts, you say?" Marvelmous was playing to the crowd. "Well, all you need is one thin dime to play."

"This may sound funny," said Luigi, picking up on Marvelmous's rhyme scheme, "but I don't have that kind of money."

"He doesn't have ten cents?" someone muttered.

"He looks like he doesn't have two pennies to rub together," sneered a nasty voice.

Luigi hung his head.

"Chin up," Professor Marvelmous whispered. "It's time to show the world who you truly are."

Curious, Luigi raised his eyes. The professor shot him a wink.

"My boy," the professor proclaimed, placing a hand over his heart as if Luigi had hurt his feelings. "Are you once again suggesting that my puzzles are simpleasy?"

Luigi played along. "They're as easy as pizza is cheesy."

The crowd moved in closer.

"Very well," declared the professor. "Take these two darts for free."

Luigi dried his sweaty palms on his jeans.

"What happens if I lose?"

"How are you at shoveling pony poop?" Marvelmous gestured to a nearby pony-ride concession. "My colleague Huck could use a hand."

Luigi nodded. "Deal."

The professor struck a very dramatic pose. "Hurl your darts! Hurl them posthaste!"

Luigi threw his final two darts.

Two balloons popped.

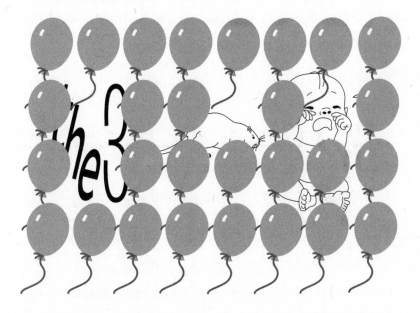

"Can you solve the puzzle, my young friend?" boomed
Professor Marvelmous.

Luigi worked it out in his head.

The. 3. Beaver. Crybaby.

No.

That made no sense.

The. 3. Muskrat? Tears?

Luigi remembered how the professor had quoted the
candy bar slogan. Had he been dropping a hint?

"Easy," said Luigi, pretending to be more confident of
his answer than he was. "The Three Musketeers."

Marvelmous acted as if he were shocked. Both hands flew melodramatically to his chest.

He whipped around and, brandishing a hat pin, quickly popped all the other balloons on the board to reveal the full puzzle.

"The. Three. Muskrat. Tears!" declared Marvelmous. "Ladies and gentlemen, boys and girls, earthlings and Martians—we have a winner!"

The crowd cheered, and more people came over to see what all the excitement was about.

"Get over here, Ronny!" someone shouted. "This game is super easy!"

"Set me up, old man!" cried another.

"I've got next!" insisted a third.

"That was brilliant," Professor Marvelmous said to Luigi, handing him the turquoise teddy bear that Chester wanted for his mom. Luigi figured that since Chester had financed his winning dart game, he should get to pick the prize. Luigi would find another way to pay back his parents for the broken mirror and window.

The professor leaned in and spoke softly so only Luigi could hear what he said next.

"Look at the crowd your antics attracted. You won so

easily, they all think they can too! Well done, me bucko. Well done, indeed."

"I didn't think I did anything special."

"This is no time for false modesty, my boy. You built tension, suspense, conflict. You turned an ordinary, ho-hum, pop-the-balloons game into a full-blown dramatic story!"

"I like games and puzzles."

"So do many others. But do you see them up here attracting a crowd? No. You do not. Nor do I. Don't hide your light under a bushel, my boy—especially one filled with apples. Quickly now. Help me blow up balloons."

"Yes, sir." Luigi turned to Chester and Bruno. "You guys? I'm gonna hang out here a little longer."

Bruno shrugged. "Suit yourself. I'm gonna go grab that funnel cake."

"You don't have any money left," said Chester.

"No. But *you* do. Come on. We'll share it."

"Okay." Chester turned to Luigi. "You sure you don't want to come with us?"

Luigi glanced over at Professor Marvelmous. The man's eyes were bugging out of his head again as he blew up balloons with the foot pump and simultaneously the old-fashioned, birthday-party way, with his mouth. Luigi couldn't explain it, but he felt like he was exactly where he needed to be.

"You guys go ahead," Luigi told his friends. "I'll see you later."

"Not if we see you first," said Bruno and Chester.

They wormed their way through the crowd of people pressing forward, eager to slap down their money and buy a few dart tosses. Professor Marvelmous raised a hinged section of the counter.

"Step inside, Luigi. Quickly, lad, quickly. I require your assistance to expeditiously deal with this unexpected crush of contestants."

Luigi hesitated for half a second, then joined Professor Marvelmous behind the counter.

"Keep pumping up balloons, as swiftly as you can."

"Yes, sir."

"I, of course, intend to pay you for your services. One dollar and sixty-five cents per hour. That's one dart more than the federal minimum wage!"

Luigi couldn't believe his ears. He was going to get paid to have fun and play games? Did it get any better than that? No, it did not.

That first hour, Luigi certainly earned his wages. People kept pushing their way up to the booth. Balloons kept popping. His ankle was sore from all the time it spent working the foot pump. Some people solved the rebus puzzles. Most did not.

Luigi could've solved them all.

Around eight-thirty, the crowds started to thin out as families took kids home to bed. Professor Marvelmous removed his banana hat and handed it to Luigi.

"Watch the booth, me bucko."

"What?" said Luigi. "Me?"

"Indeed. You are completely capable of handling the balloons, judging whether a puzzle solution is correct, and, if need be, cranking the scroll forward to the next rebus. Just be sure to honk your hat whenever something extraordinarily wondermous takes place. It's my trademark move. People expect it."

He flipped up the hinged section of the countertop.

"Where are you going?" Luigi asked, trying his best to hide the hint of panic in his voice.

"The bathroom, if you must know. Toodle-oo, I'm off to the loo. That's what they call the bathroom in jolly old England." And then the professor skipped away, humming "Skip to My Lou."

Luigi was all alone in the Balloon-centration booth.

And he had customers.

In front of him, Luigi saw a snaking line of eager players, all of them ready to turn their nickels into darts and a chance to win prizes.

There was no Professor Marvelmous to distract them and make them laugh. All eyes were on Luigi.

He wondered if this crowd would jeer and chant and throw half-empty Pepsi cups at him. But the audience seemed happy to hear whatever the new game master in the balloon booth had to say!

Luigi figured his spiel had better rhyme like the professor's did.

"Step right up and take a chance. If you win, I'll do a dance!"

"No!" shouted a voice. "Anything but that."

It was Bruno. He and Chester were way at the back of the crowd, their shirts dusted with white powdered sugar from their funnel cakes. They shot him a thumbs-up and Luigi went to work.

He raked in the coins. He passed out the darts. He kept up the snappy patter, quickly improvising rhymes, resisting the urge to pair "dart" with the most common word for passing gas. He didn't think Professor Marvelmous would appreciate it, even though Bruno and Chester sure would. But they'd decided to head home.

"You coming with us?" Chester asked. His mom's teddy bear was tucked under his arm.

"Nah. I need to stay here. Watch the booth."

"Cool," said Bruno.

Luigi waved goodbye and went back to work.

He honked the burp-squeaking bananas on his hat whenever players did something spectacular. He made up new words like "stupendelicious" and "awesometastic." He solved any puzzle any contestant claimed was impossible, like the one with a stew pot, a bag of coins with ancient symbols on them, and a couple of random letters:

"Nobody could figure that out!" said a man who had just spent enough money on darts to pop every single balloon on the board.

"Really?" said Luigi. "Why, my grandmother certainly could, because it's one of her favorite desserts. Probably because she keeps her teeth in a jar . . ."

The man narrowed his eyes and thought hard.

"Stew, *D, P,* coins, no wait—runes," he mumbled before the light bulb finally snapped on in his brain. "Stewed prunes!" he shouted. "Stewed prunes!"

"Give that man a fluffy Fred Flintstone!" declared Marvelmous, stepping out of the shadows.

"Yes, sir, Professor!" said Luigi. When the man walked away with his prize, Luigi turned to Marvelmous and said, "I'm sorry. I kind of gave him a hint."

"Pishposh. I would have done the same. The man spent, what, five dollars to clear the board?"

"Five-fifty."

"The plush toy cost me one dollar. And the look of joy on that man's face when he won? Priceless, Luigi. Priceless."

"This was fun, sir. Thank you."

"I've been watching you, Luigi. For over an hour."

"You weren't in the bathroom all that time?"

"No, Luigi. No human being can spend that much time on the toilet except certain grandparents I'm familiar with. No. I was over there. Behind the Zoltar fortune-teller machine." He gestured toward a glass booth where a turbaned automaton had one hand hovering over a crystal ball. "You have a rare gift, Luigi Lemoncello. A flair for showmanship."

"Thank you." And then, because for some reason he thought Professor Marvelmous might understand more than anybody else, he added, "I also like to invent games."

"Oh, you do, do you?"

Luigi nodded. "I have this idea for a First Letters game. It's like a secret code. You spell out a word or phrase using pictures. Cat stands for *C*. Dog is for *D*."

"Fascinating," said Marvelmous. "Sounds like oodles of fun. We should play it one day."

The professor pulled a gold pocket watch out of his waistcoat.

"It's nearly ten. The fair closes in a few minutes. Why don't you head on home and I'll see you back here tomorrow at, shall we say, three p.m.?"

"Tomorrow?"

"Oh yes. I'll be here for nine more days. I hope you will be too."

"Are you offering me a job, sir?"

"Indeed I am! Luigi, how would you like to be my apprentice? How would you like to learn everything I know about turning a simple game into a show?"

Luigi's jaw was probably hanging open. If so, he was too shocked to notice it. He didn't need to win a toaster and sell it. He would be earning money. For nine whole days!

"Thank you, sir. Thank you, thank you, thank you."

Luigi couldn't wait to race home to tell his family that he had a job. Especially his big brothers and sisters. He wasn't going to be the family oddball or weirdo anymore. He was going to be the only one with a real job that paid real money.

He ducked under the counter and was ready to race home.

"Luigi?" the professor called after him.

"Yes, sir?"

"Aren't you forgetting something?"

"Oh. Right. This is your hat."

Luigi handed him the banana hat.

"Thank you," said Marvelmous. "But what you really forgot is this!"

Professor Marvelmous popped open a tin Band-Aid box stuffed with coins and a few bills. He shook the loose coins out on the counter and sifted through them with his speedy finger.

"Huzzah! A 1942 Jefferson nickel minted in Denver. That's a keeper."

He slipped that coin into a waistcoat pocket and started sliding coins into a small brown envelope.

"Do you mind being paid in coins?" asked the professor. "I find them to be much more musical than paper currency. With coins in your pocket, you can play 'Jingle Bells' any time the mood strikes."

"Coins are fine, sir."

"Very well. Three hours at one dollar and sixty-five cents per hour equals four dollars and ninety-five cents."

"But I only worked two hours and maybe forty-five minutes."

"Didn't your mathematics instructor ever teach you about rounding up, my boy? In my book—which I haven't finished writing, by the way—two hours and forty-five minutes becomes three hours. And four dollars and ninety-five cents becomes five dollars."

Luigi's pay envelope was bulging, stuffed with quarters, dimes, and nickels.

"Now, off you go," said the professor. "Tell your mother and father you have found gainful employment. And kindly make certain that they are agreeable to our terms."

"I'm sure they will be, Professor. Thank you for this opportunity! And the money. The money will really help."

"Yes, it usually does. But, if you really want to feel rich, just count all the things you have that money cannot buy! Toodle-oo, Luigi. A domani!"

Luigi laughed. Professor Marvelmous knew a little Italian.

"A domani!" Luigi shouted over his shoulder as he ran for home.

See you tomorrow.

Dashing home from the carnival as fast as he could, Luigi burst into his family's apartment and shouted, "Guess what, everybody? I have a job!"

It was a little after ten o'clock at night. Most of his brothers and sisters were already in bed. His mother, father, and three oldest siblings were the only ones still in the living room watching TV. His dad had Saturdays off at the department store.

"A job?" scoffed his oldest brother, Tomasso. "You?"

"Yep. At the summer carnival."

"The carnival?" gasped Mary. "Did you and your friends go there to play games?"

"Maybe at first," said Luigi. "But I wound up winning a job!" He dumped all his coins on a table. "That's for the family."

"You mean for that window you made Alberto break," sniffed Mary.

"Enough, Mary," said Mrs. Lemoncello. "We all know Luigi is very sorry for what Alberto did with the slingshot."

"And the golf ball," said Fabio. "Don't forget the golf ball. . . ."

"It's five dollars' worth of coins!" Luigi explained.

Then he told his parents all about Professor Marvelmous and the balloon-pop booth and how he could have a job for nine more days, as long as the summer carnival was in town.

"Seven hours a day!" Luigi exclaimed. "Three o'clock in the afternoon until ten o'clock at night."

"That's awfully late for you to be walking home alone," said his mother.

"It's not even ten minutes away. I did it tonight. Plus, Professor Marvelmous will pay me one dollar and sixty-five cents for every hour. That means I'll be bringing home eleven dollars and fifty-five cents every night!"

His father whistled. Tomasso looked impressed. Mary was momentarily speechless.

"What're you gonna do with all that money?" asked Tomasso.

"Give it to Poppa, of course," said Luigi.

Luigi's father looked slightly embarrassed.

"Most of it," Luigi quickly added. "I mean, I'm going to pay for that broken window and mirror, but I'm not going to give you guys *all* of it. I'll keep a dollar for myself every day. So I can, you know, buy things. Pop, candy, stuff for new games."

"No more golf balls!" said his mother.

Luigi laughed and crossed his heart. "No more golf balls."

His father found his smile. "This is good, Luigi. Of course you can work for this professor at the summer carnival. And, Luigi?"

"Yes, sir?"

"Grazie."

"You're welcome."

"Exactly when does your new job start?" asked Bruno.

"Today," said Luigi. "At three."

"And you want to leave now?"

"It's not even two," said Chester.

"I know. But I want to get there early. It's my first full day."

"It's Sunday," said Bruno. "A day of rest."

"I'm too excited to rest!"

Luigi's whole body was buzzing. He couldn't sit still without squirming. And no way could he focus on the board game they were playing, hanging out in the alley.

Chester had the brand-new Milton Bradley version of Battleship. To win, you had to think and pay attention. And Luigi just couldn't do either. Not today.

"You guys want to come with me to the carnival?" Luigi asked.

"Nah," said Bruno. "I just sank his submarine, and I know where he's hiding his aircraft carrier!"

"No you do not," said Chester.

"Oh yes I do. H-seven!"

"Hit," said Chester.

"You know what'd be cool?" said Luigi as an idea flitted through his head.

"What?" asked Bruno.

"Playing Battleship in a swimming pool where you float in an actual inflatable boat and toss water balloons over the dividing wall, trying to bomb the other player!"

"Cool," said Chester. "We should definitely do that."

"Sure," said Bruno. "Right after one of us buys a mansion with a swimming pool!"

"See you guys later," said Luigi.

"Not if we see you first," said Bruno and Chester.

"My, you certainly are punctual," remarked Professor Marvelmous when Luigi arrived at the booth an hour early.

"Guess I'm just super excited," Luigi explained.

"You're also super early. Why, I'm not even wearing my banana hat."

"Want me to go fetch it for you? Is it in the trailer?"

"That's okay, Luigi. My wardrobe assistant is here today, making a few minor repairs. Apparently, I squeezed a squeaker a little too energetically yesterday."

"And you popped it out of its socket," said a freckle-faced girl with blazing-red hair who'd just come out of the back of the trailer.

She fanned one of the bananas on the hat with her hand. The girl seemed to be a year or two older than Luigi. She wore purple jeans and a billowy top embroidered with brightly colored flowers. Her headband was full of flowers too. "I glued the squeaker back into place, Uncle Clarence."

"Wondermous. Thank you, Maggie."

She turned to Luigi. "So who's this kid?"

"Ah," said Professor Marvelmous. "Maggie, I'd like you to meet my new apprentice, Luigi Lemoncello. Luigi? This is my one and only niece, Margaret—also known as Maggie—Keeley. She and her family live here in Alexandriaville."

"Pleased to meet you," said Luigi.

"Ditto," said Maggie. "You in junior high?"

"Uh, yeah. One more year."

Maggie nodded. "Guess that's why we've never met. I'm at the high school."

"Luigi has a gift for games and puzzles," said the professor. He waggled his eyebrows up and down on the word "puzzles."

"Really?" said Maggie.

"Speaking of gifts, Maggie—how are you faring with the one I gave you this morning? I was up until three a.m. tinkering with it. I had a last-minute inspiration."

"I need one of those," said Maggie. "I can't figure it out."

"My, what a pity. Toodle-oo. I need to prepare for today's show!" Grinning like he knew some sort of secret, Professor Marvelmous scampered into the trailer.

"He's your uncle?" Luigi asked Maggie when the professor was gone.

"Yeah. His real name is Clarence O'Hara. He's my mom's brother. You dig music?"

Luigi shrugged. "I guess."

"Cool."

Maggie thumbed up the dial on a transistor radio—a small black box with a silver mesh speaker—that was propped up on the counter of the booth.

A hyperexcited disc jockey babbled over a fading song.

"That's Merilee Rush doing 'Angel of the Morning' for us here on WALX. Hey, someone buy Merilee a watch! Doesn't she know what time it is?"

A duck quacked. Twice.

"Yes indeedy, WALX-keteers, it's two o'clock. Time to repeat today's riddle. We first announced it at noon, but so far no one has found the treasure!"

Riddle? Treasure?

Luigi leaned in and listened intently.

"Here we go," said the deejay. "'If you like something sweet, this is your favorite Thanksgiving treat. It's full of brown sugar and marshmallow, which makes me a very happy fellow!'"

The guy on the radio was rhyming, just like Professor Marvelmous. Luigi wondered if rhyming was a rule for clues.

"What am I," the disc jockey continued, "and, more importantly, *where* am I?"

There was a wild burst of zinging sound effects followed by the cartoon voice of Popeye saying "I yam what I yam, and that's all that I yam."

The disc jockey kept yakking over the intro to the next song. "Find today's hidden treasure and the prize is yours. And now here's Herb Alpert and the Tijuana Brass on WALX!"

Luigi grinned. He knew the answer.

"Let's go for it!" he said to Maggie.

"Huh?"

"Let's go win the radio contest!"

"You know where they hid the treasure?"

"Yeah. I think so. But we have to hurry. We need to be back here by three. I can't be late for my first day on the job!"

As they jogged along the sidewalks of Alexandriaville, Luigi turned to Maggie.

"We're looking for a can of yams," he said.

"We are?" said Maggie.

Luigi nodded. "The Thanksgiving treat with marsh-mallows on top. It's why they played that Popeye bit."

"The 'I yam what I yam' thing with the cartoon sounds?"

"Yep. Yams."

"Okay. But every grocery store has canned yams."

"Which is why they played that Herb Alpert song right after the riddle." They came to Main Street and rounded the corner. "That was our 'where' clue!"

Luigi stopped in front of a small corner grocery store. Fruits and vegetables were displayed in stacked boxes underneath a striped awning.

"Check out the name of this place." He gestured to the door.

"Herb's Fine Foods!" said Maggie. "You figured it out!" She gave Luigi an *attaboy* knuckle slug in the arm.

"Yeah," said Luigi, rubbing his arm. The *attaboy* thing stung.

Luigi led the way into the small grocery store. Slightly bent shelves, climbing up to the ceiling, sagged under the weight of canned and packaged goods.

"Can I help you kids?" asked the man behind the cash register.

"We hope so, sir," said Luigi. "We're looking for your candied yams."

The man cocked an eyebrow. "Oh, really? In July?"

"WALX sent us!" said Maggie.

The man smiled and turned up the music on the store's small radio.

"Second aisle," he said. "Bottom shelf."

Then he picked up his phone and made a call.

"Oh boy, oh boy, oh boy," said Maggie as she led the way to the canned yams.

This was something else Luigi loved about games: players got super excited the first time they realized they might actually win.

"There!" said Maggie, pointing to a can with what looked like a phony label wrapped around it: POOPEYE'S CANDIED YAMS.

"Oh, I get it," said Luigi. "Like Popeye, but wackier."

Maggie picked up the can. There was a note taped to the bottom:

CAN-GRATULATIONS FROM THE
WALX PRIZE PATROL!
TAKE THIS CAN TO THE COUNTER AS
QUICKLY AS YOU CAN.

"We won!" said Maggie, hurrying to the cash register.

"Hang on," said the man behind the counter. "Dave? You ready?" He covered the phone with his hand. "You kids are about to go live with Dave Ray on *The Dave Ray-D-O Show.*"

Maggie held out the can to Luigi. "You do it."

"Me?" said Luigi.

"You're the one who figured everything out. Besides, I hate being in the spotlight. I'm more of a behind-the-scenes person."

Before he knew it, Luigi was live and on the air. He told the disc jockey his name and where he went to school.

"Doing anything exciting this summer, Luigi?"

"You bet, Dave! I'm working at the summer carnival."

Luigi remembered how Professor Marvelmous turned everything into a theatrical bit. He needed to do the same. He was, after all, on the radio!

"So, hey, WALX-keteers," he said, trying his best to sound like the deejay, "why not pop by the Balloon-

75

centration booth and pop a balloon or two? It's more fun than popping pimples!"

Dave Ray chuckled and launched into his patter about that day's big prize, which turned out to be 144 packs of Wacky Packages bubble gum. Instead of baseball cards, Wacky Packages came with stickers for phony products like "Ratz Crackers" and "Weakies Cereal."

One hundred forty-four packs was a lot of bubble gum.

Before the summer was over, Luigi's and Maggie's jaws were definitely going to hurt.

Feeling great, Luigi and Maggie headed back to the carnival with their carton of Wacky Packages packets.

"So, Luigi," said Maggie when they reached the booth, "are you that good with puzzles, too?"

"I'm pretty good," Luigi replied with a modest shrug.

Maggie gave him a look like she was sizing him up.

Then she went to the rear of the Balloon-centration trailer, swung open the doors, and set down the carton of Wacky Packages in what looked like a storage area. Inside a clear plastic bag was a jumble of stuffed animals waiting their turn to be prizes. There were stacks of appliance boxes—toasters and transistor radios, mostly.

And there was something bulky hidden underneath a green velvet blanket.

"What's that?" asked Luigi.

"This is Uncle Clarence's gift. The one he said he was working on until three o'clock this morning."

She pulled off the shimmering fabric with a whoosh.

"Wow!" was all Luigi could say.

He found himself staring at a gleaming wooden box—a handcrafted cube, probably two feet tall, two feet wide, and two feet deep. The four sides were covered with all sorts of ornate carvings and decorative doodads. Some were swirls. Some were spirals. A few were funny faces and mythical creatures. Luigi counted sixteen chiseled rosettes—small wooden flowers—tucked into the corners of the four side panels.

There was also a brass keyhole plate centered on the top panel, but no slot for a key.

"What is it?" asked Luigi.

"A puzzle box," said Maggie.

"Not just any puzzle box!" boomed Professor Marvelmous, surprising them both. "It's the Super Puzzletastic Ten-Day Mystery Box! I've worked on it nonstop since I saw you last summer, Maggie. Why, I built it with these two hands. And a band saw. A rubber mallet, a drill, and some wood glue were also involved."

"Is there something inside?" asked Luigi.

The professor shimmied his bushy eyebrows. "I suspect one would have to open it to find out."

"But how do you open it?" asked Maggie, shaking her head.

"Ah," said the professor. "It is a puzzlement!"

"Maybe I could help you figure it out," Luigi said to Maggie.

"Wondermous!" said the professor. "I was hoping you might volunteer to assist Maggie. But, alas, it is now three o'clock. That means it's showtime!"

"Yes, sir," said Luigi. He turned to Maggie. "First thing tomorrow? We're going to figure out how to open your puzzle box!"

When Luigi stepped into the booth with Professor Marvelmous, he discovered just how many people in Alexandriaville listened to WALX. There were already two, maybe three, dozen people lined up and eager to play.

"Hey, are you the kid who found the yams at Herb's?" people kept asking him when they paid for their darts.

"Yes, indeed," Luigi answered. "I yam what I yam because I eat my yams."

His radio fans laughed as Luigi dipped into a bow and swirled a hand in front of his face.

"Free publicity is the best kind," Professor Marvelmous told Luigi as the crowd around the booth continued to swell. "Thank you for the plug on the radio. One couldn't buy advertising like that. Well, I suppose one could. But one would have to spend money to do so."

"Hey, Luigi!" shouted Maggie. "Since it's your first full day on the job, say 'cheese'!"

Luigi posed alongside Professor Marvelmous in the booth so Maggie could snap a Polaroid photo of them.

They both gestured to the wall of balloons and stuffed-animal prizes behind them. A flash bulb popped, and the camera churned out an instantly developing photograph.

Maggie waved it in the air to dry the chemicals. She'd captured the moment.

While Luigi reset the balloons, Professor Marvelmous confided in him. "I'm glad you offered to assist Maggie with her puzzle box. My niece is the most talented artist I know. She has quite the flair for fashion. Wants to study in Paris. Maybe New York. She dreams of starting her own clothing line one day, and I, for one, hope that her dream comes true. Maggie's the one who came up with my dreamy banana hat. But, alas, she has never really shared my love of puzzles."

"It's a pretty cool hat," said Luigi, securing the final balloon over the next rebus puzzle.

"'Pretty cool'?" said the professor, giving Luigi an exaggerated look of shock. "Why, it's positively awesome-tastic! Perhaps Maggie could design an article of clothing for you, eh?"

"Sure," said Luigi with a laugh. "How about a pair of banana shoes? They could burp and squeak like your hat does whenever I walk."

"Brilliant!" said Professor Marvelmous. "Dancing shoes that play their own dance music. You should speak to Maggie about this, Luigi. You should speak to her post-haste."

"I, uh, will. But not right now. Maggie went home."

The professor nodded. "She often leaves as soon as the crowds arrive. Maggie is extremely talented, but, like so many of us, she still needs to find the people who will see her for the wonder she truly is."

Luigi nodded.

He could use some people like that too.

And it would be even better if they were his brothers and sisters.

Over the next few hours, Luigi was in the thick of things. Balloons popped, puzzles were solved, and coins were collected by the score.

Professor Marvelmous kept up a steady stream of banter.

"You don't need a pickle, just one chubby nickel."

"Throw a dart, win his heart."

"Solve the mystery, go down in history!"

So many people wanted to play that Professor Marvelmous almost lost his voice. "Take over, me bucko. I will be at the nearby beverage stand sipping hot tea."

"I don't think they sell hot tea," said Luigi. "It's mostly ice-cold Coke, Pepsi, and root beer."

Marvelmous frowned and raised a finger to make a point. "Always avoid carbonated beverages whilst speaking in public, Luigi. We're barkers, not belchers. No one

83

wants to hear you burp or, for that matter, to smell what you ate for lunch! I shall scurry into town and avail myself of some soothing hot tea with honey at the Buckeye Diner. I shan't be long. Guard the fort!"

He handed Luigi the banana hat.

Luigi put it on and adjusted the brim so it had a rakish angle down to his left eyebrow. Then he struck one of the poses he'd seen Professor Marvelmous strike. Chest out. Hands on hips. He was Superman!

He tried to think of what Professor Marvelmous might say.

"Step right up and solve the puzzle. Then grab a root beer you can guzzle!"

"Whoa," said Bruno, shaking his head as he and Chester appeared at the side of the booth. "That last rhyme was a groaner, man." Bruno had powdered sugar dusting his horizontally striped shirt again.

"When'd you guys get here?" asked Luigi.

"About one funnel cake ago," said Chester.

"Huge crowd, man," said Bruno. "Congrats."

"Hey, I might need your help tomorrow," Luigi said to his friends as he handed darts to the next player. "Professor Marvelmous made this incredible puzzle box for his niece, Maggie. I told her I'd help her figure out how to open it."

"Has she tried a sledgehammer?" asked Bruno.

"There's probably a sliding panel or something," said Chester, who was more mechanically minded. "Look for the seams and grooves."

84

Luigi nodded. "That's what I'm thinking. Anyhow, that's a tomorrow job. Right now? I'm in charge of the booth!"

Bruno whistled. He was impressed.

The next dart flinger popped enough balloons to reveal a big chunk of the puzzle. But she didn't want to keep spending her money to solve it.

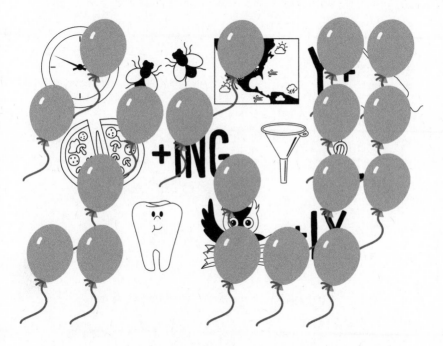

"Something about flies and a funnel and a tooth," she said. "That's all I've got. I'm done."

"Well," said Luigi, "you busted a bunch of balloons, so, just like that tooth, you're going home with something to chew on: two packs of Wacky Packages chewing gum!"

The girl laughed and took the waxy packets.

Luigi gave her a honk of his banana hat.

She moved on.

Which was when Chad Chiltington and Jimmy Willoughby pushed their way to the front of the line.

"Riffraff alert," sneered Chiltington. "It's the goofy-faced kid from your old man's apartment building."

Jimmy stepped forward, shoving a little girl who was in his way.

"What are you doing in that booth, twerp?" he demanded.

Luigi smiled and told his nerves to settle down. This was his booth. His stage. He wasn't going to let Willoughby and Chiltington ruin his night.

"What am I doing?" he said, trying his best to imitate the professor. "Hopefully, selling you two some darts before toasting myself a pair of delicious Pop-Tarts!" He gestured to the shiny toaster on the top prize shelf.

People laughed, including Bruno and Chester.

"You're working here?"

"Yes, Chad, I am," said Luigi.

"How old are you?" Jimmy asked nastily.

Luigi wiggled his eyebrows. "Why, I'm older today than I was yesterday, but not nearly as old as I will be tomorrow. Shall we celebrate? Did someone bring cake? I already have balloons."

Jimmy balled up his fist. "And I have this!"

"Hey, buddy," groused a man behind Chad and Jimmy. He was holding the hand of the girl Jimmy had elbowed. "You two gonna play or are you just here to cause trouble?"

"Trouble?" said Chiltington with his smarmy smile. "Hardly. Allow me to introduce myself. I'm Chad Chiltington. Perhaps you know my father? Chauncy Chiltington? He runs the bank."

"All I know is you're holding up the line, and your friend there bumped into my daughter without even saying 'excuse me.'"

"We're in something of a rush, old boy," said Jimmy.

"So play," grunted the man.

Chiltington slapped a pair of quarters down on the counter.

"Fifty cents!" announced Luigi. "That's good for ten darts."

Chiltington hastily hurled all ten darts at the board that was already partially cleared. He scored the same number of hits and misses. Luigi's puzzle-solving brain was already putting together some of the pieces. There was half of a pizza pie, plus "ing." That had to translate into "having," because "pizza-ing" or "pie-ing" didn't make much sense.

"Would you like to go ahead and solve the rebus?" Luigi asked Chad.

"Huh?"

"You have to figure out a phrase based on the pictures," said Jimmy. "So the first part is something like, 'Time bees weather map.'"

"That doesn't make any sense, Jimmy."

"I know. You need to pop the rest of the balloons."

Luigi knew that what Willoughby thought were "bees" were probably "flies," because "bees" could never be anything except the plural of "bee," whereas "flies" could be a verb.

But he didn't give Chad that hint.

Chiltington, the big spender, laid a crisp dollar bill down on the counter.

Luigi handed him twenty darts.

When those were gone, Luigi swept up another dollar and handed Chiltington twenty more.

Finally he uncovered the entire puzzle.

"It's something about time flying across America . . . and eating pizza," said Chiltington.

"Would you like to throw a few more darts?" suggested Luigi.

"Why? The balloons are all gone!"

"True. I just thought flinging darts might give you something to do, since you're having trouble solving the puzzle."

A few people in the crowd chuckled.

"That puzzle is impossible!" fumed Chiltington.

"Nah, it's a no-brainer," said Bruno.

"Yeah," added Chester. "It's actually quite simple."

"You two are this nork's friends!" snapped Chiltington. "You're in on the fix!"

"So how about we fix your faces?" said Jimmy, balling up his fists again.

"I'd like to see you try," said Bruno.

Oh boy, thought Luigi. *This is not good.*

The crowd pressed in tighter. They were eager to see a fight. Luigi was not.

That's when the young girl Jimmy had shoved aside spoke up.

"I can solve it," she said.

Luigi figured the kid was seven. Maybe eight.

"Please do," said Luigi.

"Go on, Alice," said the girl's dad. "Tell them the answer."

"'Time flies weather *Y* oar halving funnel knot. Chews wisely.'" Then she said it all again but faster: "Time flies whether you're having fun or not. Choose wisely."

Luigi honked his banana hat.

"Winner, winner, defrost a TV dinner! Way to go, young lady!"

The crowd cheered. Some applauded. They didn't want to see a fight anymore.

"Go ahead," said Luigi. "Pick any prize on the top shelf!"

"I want that orange dog!"

"You've got it. Chad and Jimmy? Thanks for playing. We have some lovely parting gifts for you two today. You're each going home with six packets of Wacky Packages chewing gum."

"Save it, dipstick," hissed Chiltington.

"That baseball-card gum is drier than cardboard," added Jimmy.

"It's disgusting and should be spat out," said Chiltington.

Then he leaned in closer.

"Just like you and your friends."

"All together now," said Luigi, raising his invisible sword. "Fun for all!"

"And all for fun!" shouted Chester.

Bruno, on the other hand, shook his head and said, "No thanks."

The next morning, the three friends were once again in the alley behind their apartment buildings. Luigi had invited Chester and Bruno to go with him to the fairgrounds to help Maggie figure out the solution to Professor Marvelmous's puzzle box.

"Aw, come on, Bruno," begged Luigi. "We're the three musketeers. We do everything together. You've gotta come with us."

"Why?" said Bruno. "You two already said you won't do it my way. But I'm telling you—if you want to open up any kind of wooden box, you give it a good whack with a hatchet, an ax, or, like I said yesterday, a sledge-hammer."

"But where's the fun in that?" wondered Luigi.

Bruno threw up both hands. "You guys just don't get it. You crack the puzzle box open; you get the prize inside. The prize *is* the fun. Prizes are the only reason people play games or enter contests or eat Cracker Jacks."

So Bruno would be staying home. "I have some comic books to catch up on anyhow," he said. "See you later."

"Not if we see you first," replied Luigi and Chester— but they didn't say it half as enthusiastically as they usually did. Something was off with Bruno, which meant that something was off with the three musketeers. But Luigi didn't think they should do things Bruno's way just because it might make him feel better. Destroying a magnificent puzzle box, shattering it to bits? That would make Luigi feel awful!

Luigi and Chester hiked over to the carnival grounds.

When they entered the open field with all the rides and booths, Luigi saw Maggie at the back end of the Balloon-centration trailer. She windmilled her arms over her head.

She had a backpack slung over one shoulder.

"Is that hippie girl the professor's niece?" Chester whispered.

"Yeah," said Luigi. "That's Maggie. She's very artistic. Wants to be a fashion designer."

Chester nodded. "She doesn't look like anyone I've ever seen before. I mean, not in real life. She looks like she lives in San Francisco, not Ohio."

Maggie strode across the grassy field toward them. There was a bop to her step, probably because she was listening to her transistor radio. Her braided hair bounced underneath a floppy, wide-brimmed hat. The lenses of her sunglasses were rose-colored mirrors shaped like hearts.

"Hey, Luigi," she said, and rolled her thumb down the side of the radio to click it off.

"Hey, Maggie. This is Chester. He's one of my best friends."

"Solid," said Maggie. Then she gave Chester a hand-shake that was more of a thumb-clasped fist grip.

Maggie tucked her transistor radio into a pocket of her fringed vest. "So, Luigi—there's going to be a new treasure hunt."

"Oh," said Luigi with a grin. "You want to play again?"

"No. I want to win again!"

Luigi laughed. Maggie was definitely on her way to becoming a game player.

"They won't reveal today's clue until noon," said Maggie. "So we have time to crack open my puzzle box first."

"But we won't really *crack* it open," said Chester. "That's why we didn't bring a sledgehammer."

"Cool," said Maggie. "Come on. I hauled it out of

95

the trailer. Figured we might be able to see it better in the sunlight."

Maggie led the way. Luigi and Chester followed her.

The ornately decorated cube was sitting on top of a picnic table across from the Balloon-centration booth, close to where a vendor sold hot dogs and cotton candy when the carnival was open. The lacquered wooden swirls and gewgaws shimmered in the morning sun.

"It's spectacular," said Luigi, touching its sides and admiring the intricate craftsmanship. The panels were a series of glued-together boards.

Or were they? Some of those boards might slide. . . .

"So much detail," added Chester, studying the small wooden rosettes in the corners.

"What do you think's inside?" Luigi asked Maggie.

She shrugged. "I dunno. Some kind of cool prize?"

"Probably," said Chester. "Some people say the prize is always the most important part of anything."

"I like the figuring-out part best," said Luigi, leaning in to examine the top of the box more closely. "Okay. There's this decorative keyhole. But it's just a raised brass plate. I see a tiny hole drilled into the panel beneath the plate, but the only key that would fit into it would have to be super skinny—like the width of a Tootsie Pop stick."

"Did your uncle give you any sort of hints about how to open it?" Chester asked Maggie.

"No. Just a card."

Luigi and Chester looked at each other.

"And what did the card say?" asked Luigi, because he knew you didn't present a puzzle with a card and not drop some kind of clue.

"Hang on." Maggie ran into the booth and returned with a purple envelope. She slid out the card and read what was written on it:

Maggie,
Hopefully, this puzzle box will give you
a little fun during my ten-day stay.
I like to think of it as a
countdown calendar.
But the ten doors won't open
until you find the key.
And always remember—
take time to smell the roses.

"Did you find the key?" asked Chester.

"Uh, no," said Maggie. "I even checked underneath the bottom panel. That's where I would've hidden it. Maybe with tape or something."

Luigi studied the box while Chester slid his hands along the sides, top, and bottom of the cube, searching for moving panels or loose-fitting dovetail cuts.

"I've got nothing," he reported.

"Hang on," said Luigi. He fidgeted with the round

.wooden pieces mounted in the corners of the side panels. They reminded him of birthday-candle holders and were carved to resemble roses in full bloom. "I'm taking time to smell the roses. But maybe, to do that, I need to pluck them out of the ground first."

None of the twelve flowery ornaments he fidgeted with, on three sides of the cube, budged.

But the fourth side was the charm.

One of the pieces, in a top corner, swiveled loose.

"Far out!" shouted Maggie.

The wooden rosette had been anchored into the panel by a slender peg. A peg about the width of a lollipop stick.

"This has to be something," Luigi said.

He carefully pressed the rosette's peg into the tiny hole beneath the brass key slot. He felt a slight click as it slid into place.

He gave the wooden flower a sharp twist to the right.

And the puzzle box's front panel plopped down like a castle's drawbridge.

"Wow!" gasped Maggie. "It worked! You opened the box."

Then she, Luigi, and Chester bent down to face their next challenge. Another puzzle had been hidden behind the cube's front panel.

Luigi grinned and rubbed his hands together. "And Bruno told us this wouldn't be fun."

"Who's Bruno?" asked Maggie.

"Our third musketeer," said Chester. "He thought we should just smash the box open."

"That's terrible. It's a work of art."

Chester nodded. "We agree."

"It's a sliding puzzle," said Luigi. "So we need to move these jumbled tiles around and line them up in the right order."

"And then what'll happen?" asked Maggie.

"They'll spell out a phrase, I think. Maybe it'll be our next clue."

"One step at a time," coached Chester. "It's the only way to solve a complex problem."

Luigi examined the eight sliding squares in the three-by-three grid. There was one blank space. He would need that to move the squares with letters into their proper positions to create a sentence of some sort.

"The first block, the one with 'Teacher' on it, should be up in the top left corner."

"Are you sure it's the first square?" asked Maggie.

"Pretty sure," said Luigi. "It's the only word with a capital letter, so it has to be the start of the phrase."

"Good grammar!" said Chester.

"Thanks."

Luigi had played with sliding puzzles before. Santa usually put one in each of his brothers' and sisters' stockings. Luigi helped everybody solve them on Christmas morning. Well, everyone except Mary. His oldest sister would never ask Luigi for help on anything. She thought he was silly. She thought sliding puzzles were silly too. She preferred the practical things Santa left in her stocking. Like a toothbrush or a toenail clipper.

As with most puzzles and games, there was a logical path to victory with a sliding-square challenge.

It took time, but Luigi found it.

Ten minutes later, he slipped the final square into the space where it belonged.

The phrase was complete.

"Uncle Clarence says that all the time," said Maggie. "I think it's an old Chinese proverb."

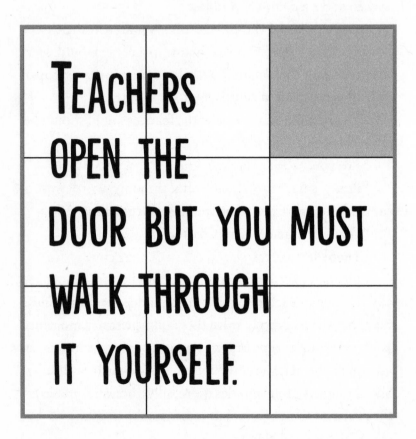

TEACHERS OPEN THE DOOR BUT YOU MUST WALK THROUGH IT YOURSELF.

A faint sound started up deep within the box.

Luigi, Maggie, and Chester all leaned in and pressed their ears against the top of the box.

They heard the distinctive *TICK-TICK-TICK* of a windup alarm clock.

"You must've activated some sort of internal timing mechanism," remarked Chester.

Suddenly, a narrow door sprang open in the back panel of the cube.

Maggie rotated the cube so they could see what was going on.

Inside the no-longer-hidden compartment was a tiny slip of paper and a small toy. Maggie reached into the cubbyhole and pulled out the note.

"What's it say?" asked Chester.

Maggie read the message:

A new door will spring open
each day of my stay.
Have fun with your prize from day one.

"This is so cool." Now Maggie pulled out a plush lion attached to a key-chain clip. "It's like I'm winning prizes at a miniature Balloon-centration booth!"

All of a sudden, there were two more pops and flops. Maggie spun the cube back around. Now two of the tiles in the sliding puzzle had flipped open.

"What day is this?" asked Chester.

"It's Monday, so it's already the third day of the carnival," said Luigi after counting on his fingers to make sure.

"So three doors sprang open to catch up with Uncle Clarence's visit!" said Maggie.

She reached into the first opening and pulled a second stuffed toy out of its secret hiding place.

"What is that?" asked Chester.

"An owl. And this one, behind door number three, is an otter! How does the box know which doors to open? How does it know what day this is?"

Luigi shook his head. "I have absolutely no idea."

"I suspect your uncle engineered a way to tell the box where it is in the ten-day cycle," said Chester. "Those ball-shaped legs on the bottom. Most likely, one of them moves. Professor Marvelmous would click it forward to let the box know what day it is. But now that you've activated the clockworks, it should tick along on its own and open a new door each day for the next seven days!"

"Is this cool or what?" said Maggie. "I mean, okay, the toys aren't huge or spectacular, but this is so much fun!"

Luigi nodded. "Bruno was wrong. The prize really isn't the important part. The fun is!"

"Oh, wait," said Maggie. "I have an idea!"

She used the key-chain clips on the three stuffed animals to hook them to the zipper of her backpack.

"Cool," said Chester.

Maggie smiled at Chester and Luigi. "Thanks for helping me figure out how to open this thing."

"It was mostly Luigi," said Chester. "He has a gift."

Luigi remembered what his sister's piano teacher had said about everybody having a gift. Was this his? Solving puzzles? If so, he wondered if he should take it back and exchange it for something better.

"You guys want one of my prizes?" Maggie asked. She started to unclip the otter. "You could dangle one off a buttonhole in your shirt."

"Um, no thanks," said Luigi. "My brothers and sisters already think I'm strange. I don't want to give them any more ammunition."

"Why not?" said Maggie. "Just be who you are, Luigi. Everybody else is already taken."

"Until tomorrow!" Maggie said to the puzzle box as she carefully returned it to its spot in the back of the trailer.

"Is it still ticking?" asked Chester.

Luigi pressed his ear against the top panel again. "Yep."

"I bet it's a Swiss clock," said Chester. "There was an article in this *Popular Mechanics* magazine I read once that said the mainsprings on some Swiss clocks are wound so tight they can run for a really long time."

"Reminds me of some people I know," joked Maggie as she tugged a shiny antique pocket watch out of her jeans.

She actually used the tiny pocket-watch pocket sewn into every pair of Levi's. Luigi had never seen anybody do that. If he did it, it would look weird. But with Maggie it just seemed cool.

"Okay," said Maggie. "It's nearly noon. Time to shift gears. You guys up for solving another radio riddle?"

"Definitely," said Luigi.

"No thanks," said Chester. "I'm going home for lunch. My mom said she'd make me a grilled cheese and Spam sandwich with Jell-O."

Luigi made a face. "On the sandwich?"

"No. The Jell-O's for dessert."

"Oh. Okay. That's a little less gross."

"And, after lunch, I'm going to hit the library. They have the new *Disney News* magazine. Mrs. Tobin said there's a story in it about the imagineers who built the Pirates of the Caribbean ride at Disneyland. I'm going to work for Disney one day."

Maggie smiled. "I'm sure you will, Chester."

"See you later, Luigi!"

"Not if I see you first!"

Chester trotted across the open field, heading for home. Luigi and Maggie went back to the picnic table. Maggie turned on her transistor radio. Then they both stared at it, waiting for the first WALX treasure-hunt clue of the day.

The music faded, and the disc jockey started his smooth spiel.

"That's Tommy James and the Shondells doing 'Mony Mony,' here on WALX!"

A duck quacked twice.

"Coming up on high noon. Time for today's riddle and your chance to win some 'money money.' We're shaking things up today. You don't have to find anything. You just have to be the first listener to turn in the correct answer to Al, the WALX duck, in our booth down at the summer carnival."

QUACK, QUACK!

"He's here?" said Maggie, looking around the deserted fairgrounds.

Luigi saw the bright yellow pop-up awning first. There was a man in a duck suit inside, sitting at a table with a WALX banner draped over it. "I'm guessing that's Al the Duck."

Maggie laughed. "It'd better be."

"Okay, here's the riddle," said the radio. "A kid was walking around at the carnival. A man called out from a booth and said, 'If I can write your exact weight on this piece of paper, you have to pay me fifty dollars. If I can't do it, I'll pay you fifty dollars.' The kid checked the booth for a scale. Didn't see one. So he took the challenge. He figured that no matter what number the man wrote, he'd just say the guy was wrong. Well, surprise, surprise, surprise. In the end, the man in the booth won the fifty dollars. How'd he do it? If you know the answer, hurry on down and tell Al in the WALX booth. If you're correct, *you'll* win fifty dollars!"

Fifty dollars? thought Luigi. That was a way better prize than all those stale slabs of bubble gum and goofy stickers they'd won the day before. Fifty dollars was a lot of money! You could use it to buy fifty gallons of milk if, you know, you really liked milk.

A new song started on the radio.

108

"We don't need to hear this," said Luigi.

Maggie scrunched up her face. "You're sure it won't be a clue, like the song was yesterday?"

"Positive. Come on."

Luigi made a beeline for the WALX booth.

"You know the answer?" asked Maggie.

"Yeah. Focus on the first thing the carnival barker said to the kid. The rest of the riddle is just a distraction—to throw you off track."

"He said he could write down the kid's exact weight?"

"Did he?" said Luigi with a wink.

They reached the booth.

The guy in the WALX duck costume was flipping through a Scrooge McDuck comic book. On the small fold-up table in front of him sat a telephone and a transistor radio tuned to 550 AM.

"Hiya, kids," said a muffled voice. "Quack, quack."

It was a very unenergetic quack. It was also a very hot day to be trapped inside a duck suit.

"Do you know the answer?"

"Yes, sir."

"Write it down on one of those cards." The duck flapped a stiff wing at a stack of WALX postcards. "If you guess correctly, you'll be going on the air live with Dave Ray!"

Luigi grabbed an index card and a pencil.

He wrote down his answer and handed it to the duck.

The duck read it and nodded at the phone. "Dial the

number you see on the clipboard there. I can't. I've got wings. You're going live with Dave Ray in thirty seconds."

Luigi felt a warm rush all over his body. If he was going on the radio, that meant he'd answered the riddle correctly!

That also meant he was going to win fifty dollars. None of his brothers and sisters had ever won fifty dollars, and he'd done it playing what Mary would call "a childish game."

And this wasn't Monopoly money. This was the real deal!

Luigi picked up the phone, dialed it, and waited for someone to pick up. Finally he heard the familiar voice of the disc jockey.

"All right, let's go live to Al the Duck at the summer carnival."

Luigi heard another QUACK QUACK.

"Oooh. Al tells me he has a winner. Put 'em on the phone, Al."

"Hi, Dave!" shouted Luigi. He was so excited, he practically shrieked it.

"Howdy, camper. With whom do I have the pleasure of speaking?"

"This is Luigi Lemoncello."

There was a pause. A very long one.

"Didn't you win yesterday?"

Luigi's heart sank.

"Uh, yes. Yes, I did."

"Well, I'm sorry, Luigi. There is a limit of one prize per listener per summer."

"Oh. I didn't know the rules. Sorry."

"That's okay. But you really can't have a game without rules. . . ."

Dave the deejay was right. But Luigi didn't want to lose this game! Or the fifty-dollar prize that would prove, once and for all, to Mary and everybody else, that playing games wasn't a complete and total waste of time.

So Luigi had to come up with a new winning strategy.

Fast!

"Next contestant?" Luigi said into the phone. "Step on up!"

"There's another contestant?" said the deejay.

"Hang on, Dave. My friend Maggie knows the answer too."

I do? a surprised Maggie mouthed to Luigi.

Luigi covered the phone with his hand.

"You know the answer," said Luigi. "It's staring you right in the face. Don't let all the extra words distract you!"

"But I'm no good in high-pressure situations."

"You can do this, Maggie."

Maggie sighed and took the phone. The guy in the duck costume shrugged. He was too hot to care whether Maggie really knew the answer or not.

She pressed the phone up to the side of her head.

"Uh, hello, Dave."

"Hi, Maggie. What's your last name?"

"Keeley. I'm Maggie Keeley."

"Okay, Maggie Keeley," said the deejay, "I'm going to repeat the riddle for any listeners who might've missed it the first time round."

Phew, thought Luigi. Maggie would have a little more time to think about her answer.

He tried to send her a telepathic message: *Pay attention! Please, pay attention!*

"Here we go," said the deejay. "A kid was at the carnival. A man called out from a booth and said, 'If I can write your exact weight on this piece of paper, you have to pay me fifty dollars. If I can't do it, I'll pay *you* fifty dollars.' The kid checked the booth for a scale. Didn't see one. So he took the challenge. But the man in the booth won the fifty dollars. How'd he do it, Maggie? What did he write on the kid's card? Get it right, and you're going home with fifty buckeroos!"

Luigi held his breath. In fact, he almost forgot how to breathe.

He could see that Maggie was thinking hard. Her face was wrinkled up so tight she looked like a raisin that had just smelled something rotten.

But then her face relaxed. A smile tugged up the corners of her mouth.

"Maggie?" said the deejay. "What did the man write on the card?"

"He wrote three words, Dave. 'Your exact weight.'

113

Because that's what the man said he'd do. That he'd write down 'your exact weight.' Get it?"

"Yes, Maggie," said the deejay with a chuckle. "I get it. Don't forget, this is *our* riddle!"

QUACK, QUACK.

"Congratulations, Maggie Keeley. You've just won fifty quackers. And, please remember—there's a limit of one prize per listener. Thanks again for playing. The summer fun continues tomorrow at noon right here on WALX!"

Maggie hung up the phone.

"Give me a second," said the duck man, peeling off his head and wings. Sweat was dribbling down his face. His hair was a soaked sponge. He flipped off the radio and handed Maggie a soggy fifty-dollar bill. Luigi figured he must've had it tucked inside his costume for a long time. But still, it was FIFTY DOLLARS!

Laughing, practically jumping for joy, Maggie and Luigi scampered away from the radio station's booth.

"Here," said Maggie, holding out the limp bill. "You take the money. I couldn't've solved it without your coaching."

Luigi was tempted to keep the whole prize for himself. Fifty dollars had to be more than enough to pay for those bathroom repairs. Then he could flash the rest of the cash in his big brothers' and sisters' faces.

Who's the goofy one now? he'd tell them. *Who's never going to amount to anything? Because, guess what? I just amounted to fifty bucks!*

But that wouldn't be fair. He and Maggie had played as

a team. And when you win as a team, you share the winnings.

"We should split it," he said.

Maggie smiled. "Okay. Deal. Let's go ask Uncle Clarence to make change for us."

They hurried over to the Balloon-centration booth, where Professor Marvelmous had just arrived.

"Hi, Uncle Clarence," said Maggie.

"Hiya, Professor Marvelmous," added Luigi.

"Greetings and salutations to you both." Professor Marvelmous pointed to Maggie's dangling backpack decorations. "And, if I may, congratulicitations upon the grand opening of your puzzle box! I take it you like your miniature carnival prizes?"

"I love 'em! Luigi and Chester helped me find the key!"

"Good for you, Luigi. And who, pray tell, is Chester?"

"One of my best friends," said Luigi.

"Well, then I am certain he shall be a friend of mine as well."

"Uncle Clarence?"

"Yes, Maggie?"

She held up the crinkled bill. "Can you break a fifty for us?"

Professor Marvelmous gasped and, once again, pretended like he might faint.

"Maggie, how on earth—or, for that matter, Mars—did you come upon such a sizable amount of cheddar, cabbage, or cake?"

"We won it from the radio," said Luigi.

"Ah! This is your second prize from WALX, correct?"

"Yeah," said Maggie. "But now I guess we're done."

"Really? Already? But you two are like cinnamon. You're on a roll."

Maggie nodded. "I know. But there's a limit of one prize per listener."

Marvelmous shook his head. "How sad it is when we must accept the limitations placed upon us by others. For instance, I hate when my pants tell me I can't eat any more chocolate cake. But, to the matter at hand. Do you two wish to split your fifty fifty-fifty?"

"Yes, sir," said Luigi.

The professor pulled out the Band-Aid box where he stored his cash. He found four tens and two fives and gave them to Maggie in exchange for the damp fifty-dollar bill.

"Promise to be thrifty with your half of the fifty?"

"Promise," said Maggie. "I'll add it to my dream fund. Paris, here I come!"

"I have big plans for this too," said Luigi, when Maggie gave him his twenty-five dollars. "I'm going to give some to my father. I owe him."

"Yes," said Marvelmous thoughtfully. "We all owe so much to our fathers. For instance, my receding hairline . . ."

Luigi laughed. "Thanks again, Maggie. I gotta run home. See you at three, Professor!"

"Guess what, you guys?" Luigi said when he got home a little before one. "I made twenty-five dollars today!"

His brothers and sisters were all sitting around the two dining room tables finishing their lunch—bologna sandwiches on white bread, with a little mustard.

"*Twenty-five* dollars?" said Tomasso with a whistle. "That's a lot of money!"

"Here, Momma," said Luigi, handing her one of his ten-dollar bills. "Will that plus the money I already gave Poppa from my carnival job be enough to pay for the stuff we broke in the bathroom?"

"Yes, Luigi," she said, sounding a little suspicious. "But how did you earn twenty-five dollars? Your job doesn't even start until three o'clock."

Luigi grinned and looked directly at Mary.

"Mom," he said, "I won it all playing a game."

Mary blew an unimpressed puff of air out of the corner of her scowl. "A *game?*"

His mother gasped. "Luigi, were you gambling?"

"No," Luigi said with a laugh. "All I had to do was figure out the answer to a riddle they asked on the radio and be the first one to tell it to a guy dressed up like a duck."

"You talked to a man dressed up like a duck?"

"It's a radio station, Momma. They do wacky stuff. First prize for the riddle contest was fifty bucks, which I split with my partner, Maggie."

"Who?" asked Tomasso.

"Professor Marvelmous's niece. She helped me win all that bubble gum yesterday," Luigi explained. "We're kind of a team. Hey, how'd you all like to be my guests at the summer carnival tomorrow?" He waved his cash in the air. "My treat!"

"No, Luigi," said his mother. "That's your money. Save it. Put it away for your college education."

"Ha!" laughed Mary. "What kind of college would Luigi go to? Clown college?"

"Enough!" said Luigi's mother.

"It's okay, Momma," said Luigi. "I can take a little ribbing. Tell you what I'm gonna do. Tonight, when I have my break, I'm gonna go buy a whole string of carnival tickets. We'll divvy them up tomorrow. You guys can ride all the rides. I'll also bring home a bag full of coins so you can eat carnival food and play some games. Hey, maybe you guys will even get lucky at my booth and win one of our top-shelf prizes."

"That'd be great," said Arianna.

"You are a very generous young man," said Luigi's mother.

"Yeah, Luigi," said Lucrezia. "Thanks."

"Tomorrow's gonna be awesome!" said Massimo.

Fusilli barked and wagged his tail. Stromboli stretched into a purr. Everybody in the Lemoncello apartment was thrilled with Luigi's offer.

Everybody except, of course, Mary.

"I don't think we should all waste our time at the carnival just because Luigi does," she said, and stuck out her tongue.

Luigi didn't care. The rest of the family thought he was a hero! And, for that one brief, glorious moment, he thought maybe they were right.

"Another one of the front tiles popped open this morning!" said Maggie when Luigi, Chester, and Bruno arrived at the fairgrounds a little before three on Tuesday. "There was a stuffed koala inside door number four!"

"Cool," said Luigi.

It was another hot and humid summer day. Luigi's shirt was glued to his back with sweat.

"This thing just opens automatically?" asked Bruno, sounding skeptical. He leaned in to examine the puzzle box in the back of the balloon-pop booth.

"It's a very cleverly designed device," said Chester.

"It's still ticking," said Maggie.

"Huh," said Bruno. "I guess, if it's true, it's pretty cool."

"Pretty cool?" said Luigi. "It's awesometastic!"

"The koala gave me an idea," said Maggie. "I'm going

to hang all my stuffed animals off the brim of this hat I'm working on."

"You make your own hats?" said Bruno.

"Yep."

"Why?"

"Why not?"

Bruno made a face and shook his head.

"I like to design stuff too," said Chester. "For instance, right now I have this idea for a pump-and-pedal bicycle. You could row its high handlebars like oars to give your ride a turbocharged boost. I've got it all sketched out."

"Really?" said Bruno. He pumped his arms in and out like he was doing a bench press while standing up. "Who'd want to buy a bike like that? You'd look like a total doofus riding it."

Chester's face reddened.

"I think it's a great idea," said Luigi. "Hey, Chester— next time you're at my house, show your sketches to my dad. He may not work at the bicycle factory anymore, but he definitely knows how to build bikes. Heck, he could build anything."

"Yeah," said Chester. "Maybe I'll do that."

Bruno shook his head. "Waste of time," he singsonged to the breeze.

"Says who-ooh?" Chester singsonged back.

"Me-eee" was Bruno's reply.

Luigi didn't like hearing his best friends sniping at each other. They were supposed to be the three musketeers. Fun for all and all for fun. He figured Bruno's grouchy mood must have something to do with the sweltering heat.

So he quickly changed the subject.

"What's your idea for this new hat?" he asked Maggie.

"I got it from the koala," she said, twirling the tiny plush toy around her finger on its key ring. "Koalas are big down in Australia. And in Australia, the ranchers wear slouch hats with corks on strings hanging off the brim."

"Why?" Bruno asked.

"They bounce around and chase away flying insects," said Maggie.

As if on cue, Chester slapped his face to swat a mosquito that had just lighted near his ear.

Luigi laughed. "You should make a bunch of them. We could all wear 'em."

"Maybe I will," said Maggie. She clipped the koala to her backpack. "See you guys tomorrow. Can't wait to see what's behind door number five!"

She popped in her transistor radio's earphone and strode across the open field.

"Wait here," Luigi said to Bruno and Chester. "I'll be right back."

He trotted off to catch up with Maggie.

"Hey, Maggie?"

"Hmm?" She had to take out the earphone to hear Luigi. "What's up?"

"There's something I've been meaning to ask you. Why don't you ever come to the carnival when it's open?"

Maggie thought about that for half a second, then shrugged. "I dunno. Too many normal people."

"Huh?"

"You know. Ordinary, average citizens. That's who *comes* to the summer carnival. Sure, Uncle Clarence and some of the other carnies are cool. But the people who play the games and ride the rides? None of them look like me. In case you haven't noticed, I don't exactly fit in. I'm fine with that, but when you don't fit in, the people who *do* fit in can be awfully mean."

Luigi could relate. He really didn't fit in with his family. Or at school. Or anywhere except maybe the alley with his friends, and the library.

"Well, maybe," he said, "you could just drop by the balloon booth tonight. I promise I won't let anybody make fun of you or your awesome new mosquito-swatting hat."

Maggie smiled. Just a little.

"I'll think about it."

"My goodness!" said Professor Marvelmous after he and Luigi had been working the booth for over an hour. "I nearly forgot."

"What?" asked Luigi.

"I forget. No, wait. I *nearly* did. Now I remember. Margaret asked me to present this to you. It's a present. She wanted to thank you for helping her unpuzzle my puzzle box."

"That smell-the-roses thing was a pretty big clue."

"Indeed it was. For *you*, Luigi. Because you are someone who pays attention and takes context into consideration. You notice things others might not."

Professor Marvelmous reached under the counter and pulled out a hatbox.

"Go on. Open it."

Luigi hesitated for an instant. But then Professor Marvelmous honked one of the bananas on his hat like a truck's air horn, to egg him on.

Luigi lifted the lid. Inside the box was a black silk top hat with a bright yellow band wrapped around the base of its crown.

"Why, it's magnificent and stupendous!" cried Marvelmous. "I daresay it's magnifendous! Put it on, Luigi. Put it on."

The hat was incredible. Like something a circus ringmaster might wear. Luigi reached for it—

Then stopped.

He thought about what he'd said to Maggie. About making sure no one made fun of *her* hat.

But still . . .

A fancy silk top hat, like something Frosty the Snowman might wear, could focus too much attention on the fact that Luigi wasn't like all the other kids in town. It could become a KICK ME sign sitting on top of his head instead of stuck to his butt.

"It might be too fancy for me" was what he told Professor Marvelmous.

"Nonsense. You're a showman. The top hat is the perfect accoutrement to show the world who you truly are."

"Um, maybe later?"

The professor nodded knowingly. "Well said, Luigi. Everything happens in its own time." He closed up the hatbox and placed it back beneath the booth's front counter.

Luigi's brothers and sisters showed up around six o'clock.

Luigi's father wasn't with them. He still had to work the night shift at Mr. Willoughby's department store. His mother didn't come either.

"She didn't want to take any of the coupons or coins away from the little kids," Tomasso explained, with a head gesture to the cotton-candy stand, where Sofia's and Massimo's faces were both covered with sticky pink strands of swirled sugar.

Everybody rode the Tilt-A-Whirl. And the Mad Mouse roller coaster. Even the Parachute Drop.

Arianna was a sport and took the younger kids on the merry-go-round.

Tomasso and Fabio spent some of their nickels and dimes swinging a heavy mallet and trying to ring the bell at the top of the strong-man game. Francesca, Lucrezia, and even Mary played the Frog Bog, slamming a seesaw catapult to launch rubber frogs into floating lily-pad targets.

Later they all came to the Balloon-centration booth.

"And who have we here?" said Professor Marvelmous, suddenly facing a wall of nine kids, all variously sized versions of his apprentice, Luigi.

"This is my family!" Luigi said proudly, even though Mary was giving him the hairy eyeball.

"Well, you're in luck, Lemoncello clan!" announced the professor as he cranked the puzzle scroll forward a few more turns than usual. "Today is Tuesday. That means family members receive *three* darts for every nickel instead of the more traditional, customary, and profitable one."

When the Lemoncellos heard that, they quickly lined up and took turns popping balloons.

"No darts for Massimo and Sofia," said Mary after she tossed one dart and burst the biggest balloon on the board. "They could put someone's eye out with these things."

"A wise and prudent call, young lady," said Marvelmous, giving her an approving toot of his banana hat.

Mary gave that one of her scowls—the kind she usually saved for Luigi.

After all his older siblings had tossed their darts, eight-year-old Alberto stepped up and threw the dart that cleared the board to reveal the complete puzzle.

"L-apple point the jockey tooth uh piggy bank!" shouted Tomasso.

"La-half awl the weigh tooth uh bacon!" tried Francesca.

Mary gasped.

"Laugh all the way to the bank!" she shouted. For a second, she was excited. She clapped and bounced up and down a few times. "Laugh all the way to the bank!"

But then she caught herself.

Professor Marvelmous honked a victorious melody on his banana hat.

"Correctamundo, my good lady, and wise advice. Why, I already did so today. I said, 'Ha-ha-ha' and then strode into their magnificent marble lobby. Now then, Lemoncellos, you may pick any prize upon my wall!"

"Take the toaster, you guys," urged Luigi. "For Momma."

"Yes!" shouted Sofia. "For Momma!"

"For Momma!" shouted all the rest. Mary joined the chorus, but not quite as loudly as the rest.

Luigi handed Tomasso the toaster.

"Thanks," said Tomasso. "This is fun."

Luigi felt fantastic. Here at the carnival, he wasn't the family oddity. He was the fun-maker!

"Come on, you guys," said Alberto. "I've still got some tickets left!"

"Me too," shrieked Arianna. "Thanks, Luigi!"

Professor Marvelmous watched all the Lemoncellos race off to find their next amusements. "Families are like branches on a tree, Luigi," he said. "We grow in different directions, but our common roots remain."

Then his voice brightened. "And speaking of family, here comes my wondermous niece!"

Luigi's smile went wide.

Maggie had taken his suggestion.

She'd come to the carnival.

And she was wearing her brand-new hat!

Each of the miniature stuffed animals from the puzzle box's secret compartments was dangling off Maggie's handmade, flat-brimmed felt hat.

It was a look all her own. And she was right. She definitely did not fit in with the crowd milling around the fairgrounds.

"So good to see you, my dear!" cried Professor Marvelmous. "To what do we owe the honor of this special guest appearance?"

Maggie nodded toward Luigi. "Your apprentice invited me."

"I see, I see." The professor wiggled his fuzzy caterpillar eyebrows. "Well then, I'll leave you two to it. Luigi? You're in charge of the booth. I need to take a short intermission. Toodle-oo, you two! Toodle-oo!"

He raised the hinged flap in the counter and bustled across the fairgrounds to the porta-potties.

"He needs a lot of bathroom breaks," Luigi whispered to Maggie. "He drinks a lot of tea."

Maggie tossed back her head and laughed. When she did, the stuffed animals hanging off her hat swung and swayed like Christmas tree ornaments after the cat attacks the tree.

Luigi pulled fifty cents out of his pocket and dropped the coins into the money tray. "Your first darts are on me!" He handed her ten darts.

And then he froze.

Because a sweaty group of big, preppy boys had just arrived.

"Take that ridiculous hat to the back of the line. It's my turn to play."

It was Chad Chiltington.

Jimmy Willoughby, of course, was right there with him. So were five or six other high school guys, some in plaid shorts, some in pastel-colored polo shirts. All of them doing whatever they could to look mean and tough.

And right behind them?

Luigi's sister Mary. She looked terrified.

Chiltington slapped a ten-dollar bill down on the counter. "Load me up. That's enough for two hundred darts."

"Sorry," said Luigi, his voice cracking slightly. "It's Maggie's turn."

"Says who?" said Jimmy Willoughby.

"The rules," replied Luigi. "After all, this is a game! And without rules, what are games except a collection of cardboard, plastic, and dice? Or, in this instance, balloons and darts."

He needed a distraction. Something to pop the tension in the crowd the way a dart pops a balloon.

He turned to Maggie. "Will you excuse me for a moment?"

He ducked down, opened the hatbox, and slid out the silk top hat.

Still crouching, he pulled the hat down on his mop of curly hair.

Something about it made him feel special.

No, the professor had been right. It made him feel like the showman he wanted to be.

"And," said Luigi, rising up with his somewhat-too-big-for-his-head top hat riding low on his ears and his finger pointing dramatically skyward, "the very first rule of any game is who plays when."

"You tell 'em," said Maggie.

"Oh, I intend to," Luigi said with a smile. "In Sorry, the youngest player goes first, and play passes to the left. In Monopoly, each player throws the dice, and the player with the highest total starts the game. In Chutes and Ladders, you must first spin the spinner, and the highest spin will, henceforth and hencefifth, spin first."

Now the people in the gathering crowd, the ones who

weren't with Chiltington and Willoughby, started smiling and laughing.

Luigi kept going. "Well, here at the Balloon-centration booth, we have our own rules of fair play, since these are, after all, the *fair*grounds, and our rules read as follows, so please follow along: 'The person at the front of the line, also known as the first person in line, goes first.'"

"Who exactly do you think you are, kid?" demanded Chiltington.

Luigi gave him a tip of his top hat. "I, sir, am Luigi L. Lemoncello. Now, kindly step back. Madam? If you please. Hurl away!"

There was a little sweat on Luigi's upper lip, but his voice was steady and strong. He looked up and realized he had attracted a small audience. He could see Tomasso, Fabio, and Francesca licking ice cream cones. And Mary was still glued to her spot. All four were staring in disbelief as Luigi took total command of the situation.

This was what he was meant to do.

This was who he was meant to be!

And no way was he going to let Chad Chiltington or Jimmy Willoughby stop him!

"Stand back," said Maggie, picking up the first of her ten darts. "Let me show you how it's done."

She took aim, limbered up her arm, and let the dart fly.

A balloon popped and revealed the first part of the rebus puzzle.

"Hey, do you always dress like that?" sneered Chiltington. "Or did you think today was Halloween?"

His friends laughed.

Maggie ignored them all and fired another dart.

BAM! Another balloon exploded.

"We don't really want weirdos in Alexandriaville," said Willoughby.

Maggie took in a deep breath and flung two darts in rapid succession.

BAM-BAM.

Two more balloons disappeared.

"Whoa," Luigi heard one of the burly high school guys behind Chiltington and Willoughby say. "She's good."

"Shut up, Todd," seethed Chiltington.

Meanwhile, Willoughby kept badgering Maggie. "And what's up with that hat?"

"Oh, it's just something those of us in show business like to wear," said Luigi, gesturing to his silk top hat.

"I was talking to her."

"Well, perhaps you should stop," said Luigi. "Because I don't believe she's listening."

"I'm not," said Maggie. "I'm throwing darts. But keep talking. Maybe one day you'll say something intelligent."

"Oooh!" said another one of the high school guys. "Zinger!"

In a flourish, Maggie hurled the rest of her darts.

"Would you like to solve the puzzle?" Luigi said to Maggie. He gestured grandly toward the balloon board.

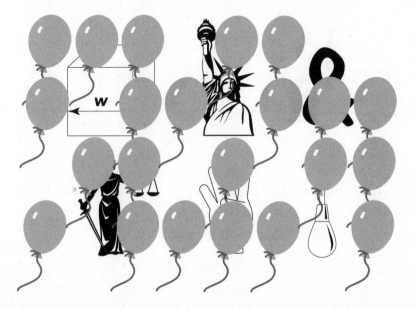

"Not yet."

Maggie kept her eyes locked on the parts of the puzzle she'd revealed.

"Give me ten more darts, please."

"Come on," whined Chiltington, waving his ten-dollar bill at Luigi. "Give someone else a turn."

Maggie slapped two shiny quarters on the counter. Luigi gave her ten more darts.

With ten quick flicks, she popped ten more balloons.

"Whoa!" said the clump of guys behind Chad and Jimmy. They were impressed.

"Would you like to solve the puzzle?" Luigi asked.

"Yeah," said Maggie. "I would."

"Very well. What does the puzzle say?"

Maggie mumbled a little as she worked through the pictures. "Width. Statue of Liberty. And. Blind-justice lady. Four fingers. Some kind of tool . . ."

"It's an awl," said the guy named Todd.

Chiltington whipped around to glare at him.

Maggie grinned a sideways grin. "Of course it is. Thanks, Todd. Because the puzzle says, 'With liberty and justice for all!'"

Luigi heard a familiarly happy honk and toot.

Professor Marvelmous climbed back into the booth, pumping his banana hat.

"Well done, young lady! Why, that was some of the finest flicking and flinging of dazzling darts that I have e'er witnessed. Which prize would you like, my dear?"

"How about that fluffy little lamb?"

"The fluffy little lamb it is!" boomed Luigi, using a pole to pluck the stuffed toy off its hook.

"Thanks," said Maggie, giving her plush prize a good hug. "For everything."

Luigi gave her a wink. "You're welcome."

"My, what a crowd!" said Professor Marvelmous, oblivious to the daggers Chad Chiltington was shooting at him with his eyes. "Who's next?"

"I believe Mr. Chiltington here," said Luigi.

"Very well," said Professor Marvelmous. "Step right up, young man."

Chiltington made a big show of stuffing his ten-dollar bill back into the pocket of his jeans.

"Nah. That's okay, old man. We don't want to waste our money trying to win any of that cheap garbage you've got hanging on your wall." Then he looked Luigi in the eye. "Besides, we're all done playing games. From now on? Things are gonna get serious. Real serious."

Early the next day, Luigi returned to his happy place.

The summer-carnival fairgrounds.

He was wearing his silk top hat with the bright yellow band. He liked the way it made him feel. Now he wanted to be at the balloon booth when the puzzle box popped open its fifth door.

Its fifth door.

The summer carnival was only in Alexandriaville for ten days. It was now, officially, halfway over. That meant his job with Professor Marvelmous was also halfway done.

What would Luigi do next?

He decided to worry about that later.

Soon. But later.

Maggie met him at the trailer.

"Did another door open?" he asked.

"Yeah," said Maggie.

"Aw. I missed it."

"You didn't miss much. Today's surprise was a weird one."

She showed Luigi her palm. There were four pennies in it.

"That's all?"

"Yep. I was, you know, expecting another toy."

"Me too. What's up with the four cents?"

Maggie shrugged and slid the coins into a pocket. "I dunno. Maybe Uncle Clarence wants me to go buy four gumballs out of a gumball machine."

"Ugh," said Luigi. "No more gum. My jaw still hurts from trying to chomp that stiff stuff from the Wacky Packages."

"Mine too," said Maggie. "Nice hat."

"Thanks." He adjusted it slightly. "So, you want to come with me to the library? I need to figure out my next gig."

"Your next gig?"

"Yeah. What do I do when your uncle Clarence leaves town?"

"Uh, how about going back to whatever you were doing before?"

Luigi shook his head. "Nah. I need to keep moving forward. Ever upward."

"And why the library?"

"It's where I do my best thinking."

While Luigi and Maggie were chatting, he noticed something over at the far edge of the fairgrounds: the silhouettes of two guys on bikes. They were backlit by the blazing morning sun. Luigi wasn't certain, but they sure looked like Chiltington and Willoughby.

He remembered what Chiltington had said at the booth. The look in his eyes when he'd said it. *We're all done playing games. From now on? Things are gonna get serious. Real serious.*

"Come on," Luigi said. "We need to go. Now."

Maggie laughed. Her back was to the boys on bicycles. "Why the rush?"

"Because I only have five days to figure out my next big thing!" said Luigi.

They left the carnival.

Fast.

Fortunately, the two boys on bikes didn't follow them.

"Guess I shouldn't wear this indoors, huh?" Luigi said to Mrs. Tobin when he and Maggie entered the library.

He still had on his top hat.

"Well, Luigi," said the librarian, "as attractive as I find your chapeau, it is considered polite to remove one's hat when entering a home. And this library is home to all the knowledge in the world."

Luigi took off his hat and hung it on a hook at the top of the coatrack.

"The hat came in handy last night," Maggie told Mrs. Tobin.

"How so?" she asked.

"It made Luigi look very official, standing inside the balloon booth."

"Well," said Mrs. Tobin, "sometimes the right article of clothing can make anyone feel fearless."

"I know. It's why I like fashion so much."

"Then," said Mrs. Tobin, "be sure you spend some time with the fashion-design books. Dewey decimal number 746.92."

"Okay. How do I find that number?"

"Follow me."

Maggie and Mrs. Tobin went off to explore the bookshelves. Luigi retrieved the boot box the librarian let him keep in a storage closet. He placed it on a table in the reading room. Inside was a taped-together game board (made out of the cardboard backs of writing pads), several marbles, some dice, and a stack of handwritten cards.

"What's all that?" asked Maggie when she came back into the room with a big book about the history of fashion.

"It's a prototype for a board game I've been tinkering with."

"Looks . . . interesting."

"Mrs. Tobin lets me fiddle with it here at the library."

Maggie examined the game board—four flaps of thin cardboard held together with Scotch tape. On one side, Luigi had glued graph paper and drawn a snaking path broken down into squares.

"It's my Kooky-Wacky Five Hundred Race Car game," he explained. "That's the course. These marbles are the race cars."

"Don't they just roll off the game board?"

"Yeah. One day I'm going to buy some Matchbox cars or a few of those brand-new Hot Wheels for playing pieces. But toy cars cost money. . . ."

"Which you're now making."

"True. Anyway, you roll the dice to move your car around the racetrack. Some of the spaces give you bonuses— like a zoom square. That means you get to zoom past your opponents by rolling again. Or you could land on a clunker square."

"A clunker?" said Maggie.

"Something bad happens. You skid out and go back three spaces. Or your engine drops out so you lose a turn. This one is a flat-tire square."

"You lose another turn?" said Maggie, catching on.

"Exactly. Oh, here's my favorite space." Luigi tapped a square filled in with bright green crayon slashes. "It's green. For Flubber."

"Like in that movie?" said Maggie. "*The Absent-Minded Professor*?"

"Yep. You land on the Flubber square, your car can fly!"

"So you basically win?"

"Unless"—Luigi tapped a square with a cartoon of a googly-eyed squirrel—"your opponent lands on the angry-flying-squirrel square. Then watch out."

Maggie and Luigi hadn't noticed Vinny Ciccarelli slipping into the reading room to peer over their shoulders.

The shy boy tapped Luigi on the arm.

"Oh hey, Vinny. This is my friend Maggie."

Vinny nodded and pointed at the taped-together cardboard flaps. "What's that?" he mumbled.

"It's a board game I've been working on. But it doesn't really work. It needs toy cars. Or, wait a second— we could borrow the race-car tokens from everybody's Monopoly sets!"

"Or . . . ," whispered Vinny.

"Or what?"

Vinny pointed to the window.

"You could play outside," he said very softly. "The sidewalk has squares. Just like your game board."

"Neat idea, Vinny!" said Luigi.

He was excited. The sidewalk board game would be a blast. It'd be simple to set up, and he could charge players an admission fee—say, fifty cents. He could still make money while having fun.

"We can take chalk and turn a whole block into the board," he said. "We'll make a giant number spinner, since dice would just disappear out on the sidewalk."

"We could collect hats!" said Maggie. "Baseball caps. Different colors. People put on a cap and become a playing piece."

"We could rig up a zip line for the Flubber and flying-squirrel squares," said Luigi. "Chester could be in charge of that."

"Whoa!" said Maggie. "Everybody's going to want to land on those two squares. It'll be a blast!"

Luigi turned to Vinny. "Vinny, you're a genius."

Outside, a horn honked.

"Thanks," said Vinny. "Bye." He jabbed a thumb toward the window. "Mom." He dashed out of the reading room.

"Kid doesn't say much, does he?" remarked Maggie.

"Nope."

"I can relate. I'm not super chatty around people either."

"Um, I'm a person."

"True. I guess it's crowds I don't like. I could never do what you and Uncle Clarence do. But back to the sidewalk board game . . ."

"Oh, you mean the First-Ever Sidewalk Board Game Extravaganza!"

"Right," Maggie said with a laugh.

"I'll ask Bruno and Chester to help us out."

"Help you out with what?" said Bruno as he and Chester strolled into the reading room.

Bruno went straight to the window air-conditioner unit and flapped up the bottom of his T-shirt. "It's a scorcher out there."

"You guys?" said Luigi. "Vinny gave me this idea for an outdoor board game based on my Kooky-Wacky car game. We turn the squares of the sidewalk into spaces on the board. Chester? Can you set up a zip line for the Flubber and squirrel squares?"

"Yeah. I think so. Your dad has a bunch of wheels and cables and pulleys and stuff down in the building's basement. The super has tools in his shed. We're using them to build that bike I sketched up."

"You're kidding," said Bruno. Now he was trying to blast air-conditioning up into his armpits. "You two are actually building that bike?"

"Yep," said Chester. "I showed Mr. Lemoncello my drawings. He says I have a real talent for mechanical engineering."

"You do," said Luigi. "I knew he'd love that pump-and-pedal idea."

Over by the window, Bruno shook his head. "Well, I've got some ideas about stuff I want to make too."

"Like what?" said Chester.

"A sandwich. With three kinds of meat."

"You guys?" said Luigi. "Can we focus on the sidewalk board game?"

"Sure," said Chester eagerly.

"Whatever," said Bruno. He didn't sound quite as eager.

Luigi plowed ahead anyhow. "I think we should do it this Saturday. So we only have three days to set everything up."

"Um, can we wait to start until after noon?" suggested Maggie. "I want to play that radio game again."

"So you can win more of that nasty bubble gum?" said Bruno.

"Or maybe," said Chester, "another fifty bucks."

"But we've already won," Luigi reminded Maggie. "And there's that limit of one prize per listener. I thought that was why we stopped playing."

Maggie pursed her lips. "It was. But I miss the excitement. The thrill of the hunt!"

"We could win," said Chester. "Me or Bruno."

Maggie brightened. "That's what I was thinking. You can have the prize. I just want to go along for the ride."

"You do it, Chester," said Bruno. "I don't want to play any game unless I know what the prize is." He turned to Luigi. "Speaking of which, what's the prize for this sidewalk board game?"

"I haven't figured that part out yet."

"Well, you better. I keep telling you—the prize is the most important part of any game. It's the only reason people play. I gotta go. We're having SpaghettiOs for lunch." Bruno headed for the door. "And with SpaghettiOs I know what I'm getting. Spaghetti. Shaped like Os."

"See you later!" cried Luigi, Chester, and Maggie.

But, for the first time ever, Bruno didn't say anything in reply.

Luigi put all the pieces for his prototype game back into their box. Chester helped.

"I promise we'll take Thursday and Friday off from the radio contests so we can focus on the sidewalk board game," said Maggie.

Luigi nodded. "That should give us plenty of time."

"Cool!" said Maggie.

The three friends said goodbye to Mrs. Tobin and headed to the curb. Maggie dug her transistor radio out of her backpack and found room inside to stow Luigi's top hat.

It was nearly noon.

Maggie turned up the volume.

QUACK! QUACK!

"It's time for today's treasure-hunt clue," said the deejay. "Here we go. 'Approach this bench outside to see the time. Approach the bench inside to see if you're doing time.'"

A snare drum and banjo started playing.

"Happy treasure hunting! Comin' at you, the Royal Guardsmen with their chart-climbing new single, 'Snoopy for President,' on WALX!"

"Come on, you guys," said Chester.

"Where are we going?" asked Maggie.

"The county courthouse!"

The Buckeye County Courthouse was only five minutes away from the library. Lots of other eager listeners were already swarming the grounds. Some were poking around under park benches. Some were searching in trash cans. Some were badgering the guy sitting in the WALX Prize Patrol van.

Two were straddling their bikes at the corner of an intersection.

"It's those guys from last night," said Maggie.

Luigi nodded. "Chad Chiltington and Jimmy Willoughby."

"Are they following you?" asked Chester.

"Maybe."

"Or maybe they just listen to WALX," said Chester, sounding excited. "Whatever we're looking for is over near that park bench."

"Shhh!" said Luigi. "Everybody else is looking for it too, remember?"

"Right. Sorry."

"How can you be sure it's by the bench?" Maggie asked Chester.

"Because," Chester whispered, "it's the only bench you can sit on and look straight at the clock in the tower!"

Luigi picked up the thread. "And the clue said, 'Approach this bench outside to see the time.'"

"Right," said Chester. "The other clue about the bench inside and doing time gave us the general courthouse location."

"You guys are good, man," said Maggie.

She was the first to notice the doghouse-shaped lunch box lying in the grass beside the bench. "Have Lunch with Snoopy" was printed across its latched lid.

"Chester?" she whispered. She nodded toward the lunch box.

"Hmm?"

"'Snoopy for President'?"

Chester shrugged. "Yeah. That song's pretty good, but—"

His eyes went wide. Luigi grinned.

Whistling, Chester casually strolled toward the Snoopy lunch box and nonchalantly picked it up. He snapped open the lid. Inside was a note instructing the winner to "go see the man in the van."

"I won!" Chester shouted. "I WON!"

"See?" said Maggie. "I told you. Winning is fun."

"Fun? It's amazing!"

They hurried over to the WALX Prize Patrol van.

Chester went home with a coupon good for four free lunches at the Buckeye Diner.

Bruno would've loved it.

"Don't bother hiking over to the trailer this morning," Maggie told Luigi on the phone first thing Thursday. "Guess what was behind door number six? One penny!"

"You're kidding," said Luigi. "Maybe your uncle ran out of stuffed animals."

"Or maybe he thinks I want to be a coin collector like him. All those pennies, nickels, dimes, and quarters he scoops into his money tray every night? He examines them all. It's his hobby."

"Huh. Was the one in the treasure box a rare penny?"

"I don't think so. It was shiny and new. So were the four from yesterday."

"Weird."

"Yeah. Guess weirdness just runs in my family. Anyhow, I'm going to head over to your place. Help you guys work on the sidewalk board game."

"Great! Chester and my dad are already dragging a bunch of metal junk into the alley for the zip lines. Then Dad's gonna finish building Chester's bike. He has a welding torch, goggles, the works. Since they don't need him at Belkin Bikes anymore, he says maybe he'll just start his own bicycle factory!"

When Luigi hung up, Mary was in the kitchen, glaring at him.

"What are you cooking up now?" she demanded.

"A fun game. Something for the whole neighborhood. It might even make us some more money."

He shot Mary a wink.

She gave him a withering eye roll.

Maggie walked over to Poplar Street and helped Luigi scrounge together sidewalk chalk, baseball caps, and poster board.

Together they went door to door in the apartment buildings, seeing if anybody had school or craft supplies to spare. All the neighbors pitched in what they could. Luigi promised them "fifty percent off" the price of admission. They all said they'd be there on Saturday morning for the big game.

Around noon, while Chester and Mr. Lemoncello worked on their bicycle project, Luigi, Maggie, and even Bruno (who said he didn't have anything better to do) drew their first game-board square with bright purple chalk on the concrete sidewalk.

"This looks good," said Luigi, admiring his handiwork.

"Fill in the letters with yellow," suggested Maggie.

"You figure out the prize yet?" asked Bruno.

"Well, if we charge fifty cents to play," said Luigi, "maybe the winner of every race gets a buck."

Bruno nodded thoughtfully. "You double your money. That'll work."

"You guys?" said Maggie. "We have a couple of uninvited guests. Again."

She nudged her head toward the stop sign at the end of the block, where two boys lurked on their bikes.

Chad Chiltington and Jimmy Willoughby.

Luigi's whole body tensed. He stood up and dusted the chalk off his hands.

"Can we help you two?" he shouted up the street.

"How come you guys keep following us?" added Maggie.

"Because somebody needs to keep an eye on you weirdos!" said Chiltington.

"What happened to your hats?" asked Willoughby. "They made you look even goofier than you already do!"

Bruno gave the older boys a look that might've terrified guys twice their age. "How'd you two like a knuckle sandwich?"

"Ha!" scoffed Chiltington. "Who's going to give it to us?"

"Me!" said Bruno. He clenched his fists and chased after the two bike riders.

They sped away.

If they hadn't been on bikes, Bruno definitely would've delivered those sandwiches he'd promised.

That night at the summer carnival, Professor Marvelmous told the crowds about "the First-Ever Great Sidewalk Board Game Extravaganza!"

After every winning dart game, he would launch into a sales pitch.

"Ladies and gentlemen, boys and girls, buoys and gulls. If you enjoyed your time popping balloons with us this evening, be sure to pop by Twenty-One Poplar Lane first thing Saturday morning. My young apprentice, Luigi L. Lemoncello, has cooked up something extra special, and it isn't spaghetti with chili and shredded cheese on top. Oh, no. This is even better. You won't be bored playing Alexandriaville's first and only outdoor board game, for it will be like me: simply marvelmous! What's the cost of admission, you might ask, just as I am doing right now?"

He turned to Luigi.

"Fifty cents!" Luigi shouted.

"And what does the winner win?"

"Pride, glory, and double the cost of admission!"

The crowd cheered.

"Is it gonna be fun?" someone hollered.

"Fun?" said Professor Marvelmous, pretending to be shocked. "Hello? It's a Lemoncello!"

The crowd laughed and applauded. Luigi took a slight bow.

"See you on Saturday!" he shouted, tipping his hat to his audience.

Things were definitely looking up.

With all the free publicity at the summer carnival, Luigi knew his sidewalk board game would be a big hit.

Things were also looking up inside the mystery box. On Friday morning, the seventh day of its run, a door popped open to reveal a new stuffed animal. A miniature meerkat.

"Guess Uncle Clarence ran out of pennies," Maggie joked.

And then she clipped the dangling meerkat onto the brim of her bug-swatting hat.

All day Friday, Luigi and his friends continued setting up the sidewalk board game.

"Move the spinner over here," said Chester, pointing to the curb in front of 21 Poplar. "We can lean it up against the fire hydrant."

Luigi and his friends had executed Chester's design for what he called the Spin-o-matic 5000. It consisted of a round garbage-can lid, some wing nuts, a few two-by-fours for the frame, and a rusty ONE WAY arrow sign Bruno had hanging in his bedroom. (He'd found it years ago in a junkyard.) Maggie painted ten colorful slices on the lid. Most were numbers. One was "Lose a Turn." Another read "Spin Again."

"Question," said Chester, raising his hand as if they were all in school. "How will players be able to spin the

Spin-o-matic after they move away from the starting line and head up the block and across the street?"

"I'll be the official spinner," said Luigi. "I can spin and call out numbers."

Luigi showed everybody his map of the game's layout.

"The crosswalk at the end of the block will be a free slide."

"Should we oil it down?" suggested Bruno. "Make it slick like a Slip 'N Slide?"

Luigi considered this. "Might be too dangerous. For little kids and old folks."

"Ah, everything's too dangerous for them," Bruno grumbled.

Luigi continued explaining the board's layout. "When you reach the end of the block, you cross the street and head down the squares over there. The next crosswalk is another free slide that brings you back over here, where you race up this side of the street and cross the finish line, which is the same as the starting line."

"We should have a checkered flag," said Bruno.

"I'll make one," said Maggie.

"I'm ready to set up the zip line for the Flubber and flying-squirrel squares," said Chester, tugging the cable, pulley assembly, and handle grips out of a cardboard carton.

Most of Luigi's brothers and sisters were also pitching in and lending a hand. Luigi had promised to split his share of the day's take with all his siblings.

"I'll help Chester with the zip line," said Luigi's oldest

brother, Tomasso. "Dad talked me through it. I'll also test it out. First. Before anybody else rides."

Everybody was laughing and shouting and asking questions.

Tomasso had a blast test-flying the zip line. Ten times.

Luigi's other brothers and sisters helped chalk in the sidewalk squares and had fun scrawling things like "Oil Spill," "Wipe Out," and "ZOOM! Spin Again" in thick strokes on the sidewalk's crackled concrete squares.

Well, everybody was having fun except Mary.

"Luigi, I have a question," she said with a smug smile. "What will you do if it rains between now and tomorrow morning?"

Mary seemed to enjoy the idea of Luigi's big day being ruined.

He thought for a second about what she'd said. About how even a quick summer thunderstorm could wash away all the chalk and hard work. How nobody would want to play an outdoor game on a rainy Saturday morning. But Luigi wasn't going to give Mary the satisfaction of letting her know he *was* worried about the weather.

Instead he put on an act.

"If it rains," he said melodramatically, "why, I'll weep like the clouds above. And then, Mary, I'll improvise. I'll make something up. I'll take life's lemons and make lemonade, for never forget—I am a Lemon-cello!"

Mary closed her eyes and shook her head. Then she walked away.

Fortunately, Saturday dawned bright and sunny.

Maggie found another miniature plush toy behind door number eight of her puzzle box: an ostrich. She and Luigi agreed: the puzzle box wasn't nearly as exciting as it had been when they'd first figured out how to open it. Now it felt like a self-winding vending machine spitting out tiny toys or coins at regular intervals.

A huge crowd turned out for the sidewalk board game.

"This is so exciting," Mrs. Lemoncello told Luigi. "I'm going back upstairs to make lemon-berry fizz for everybody!"

Contestants lined up, eager to hand Bruno their fifty cents for admission. Collecting money seemed to make him happier than he had been in days.

Luigi was the master of ceremonies, decked out in his top hat, a bow tie, and a bright yellow tailcoat and checkerboard vest that Maggie had made.

"Ladies and gentlemen, boys and girls, spectators and tater tots," he declared, "welcome to the Kooky-Wacky Five Hundred!"

Vinny, the quiet boy from the library, had biked over to watch the action. He had one of those battery-powered *V-RROOM!* Hot-Rodder Engines from Mattel mounted on his ride. He throttled it up and down near the starting line to make engine noises at the start of every race.

Clumps of six players, each one in a different color

hat, took turns twirling the Spin-o-matic to determine who went first in their group, since that, of course, was the first rule of any game. Then they blasted off.

Everybody was laughing and cheering. Luigi soaked it all in. His sidewalk board game was a hit. He felt a hundred times better than he had when he'd unveiled his First Letters game at the dinner table.

He couldn't wait to tell Professor Marvelmous all about it. The professor had asked Maggie to give Luigi his regrets for not attending "today's festivities."

"It's in the morning," she'd told Luigi. "Uncle Clarence isn't really a morning person."

Bruno bustled over with a shoebox filled with cash and coins.

"We've already made over fifty bucks!" he reported. "And it's not even noon!"

The street was filled with parents and kids—whole families—some from the neighborhood, some from the carnival. All of them eager to pay and play.

Nobody landed on Flubber until early in the afternoon.

"I'm Lily Morel, and I can fly!" shouted the girl who was the first to hit the zip-line square.

She grabbed on to the handle, took a running start, pulled up her feet, and flew past all the competition. Vinny gave Lily a triple *V-RROOM!* when she landed one square away from the finish line.

Luigi doffed his top hat to the girl, swirled it in front of his face, and bent into a bow.

Where he remained frozen.

A police cruiser had just crawled up the crowded street. It made everybody step back and move out of its way.

The police car *BLOOP*ed its siren once and swirled its domed red roof light as it crept to a stop.

An officer climbed out from behind the wheel.

"Who's in charge here?" he asked.

Everybody pointed to Luigi.

The kid in the top hat and bright yellow tailcoat.

"Nice to see you, sir," Luigi said to the police officer.

Luigi was so nervous, his knees were trembling.

"What's going on here?" the officer asked.

"It's, uh, a sidewalk board game. You see, you spin the Spin-o-matic . . ."

"This thing blocking the fire hydrant?"

"Uh, yes, sir. It's a spinner. For a race-car game."

Vinny slid the plastic throttle on his battery-powered noisemaker up and down.

V-RROOM! V-RROOM!

It didn't help.

The police officer squinted at Luigi. "Where are your parents?"

"My dad is at work," said Luigi. "At the movie theater. They had an early show this morning."

"What about your mother?"

"She's upstairs making lemon-berry fizz," offered Mary, who'd hurried over the instant she sensed that Luigi was in trouble. "Would you like me to go fetch her, Officer?"

"Yes."

Mary ran up the stoop and into the apartment building. "Momma? Momma? Luigi's in trouble! Again!"

Just then, a convertible flanked by two bikes crunched up the street. Luigi recognized the driver: Mr. Hannigan, owner of Hannigan Drugs on Main Street. He was also the mayor of Alexandriaville.

And of course Luigi recognized the two bike riders. Chad Chiltington and Jimmy Willoughby.

"Hello, Officer Wozniak," said the mayor, easing his convertible to a stop.

"Mayor" was all Officer Wozniak said in reply.

"Is everything under control?"

The police officer shrugged. "Kids just seem to be having some fun playing a game."

"Officer?" said Chad Chiltington, smiling politely. "I'm sure a law-enforcement representative such as yourself is very familiar with what we'll call this town's 'rule book' and the class B civil offense associated with 'encumbering a street or sidewalk.'"

"That sidewalk definitely looks encumbered," Jimmy tossed in.

"Then there is the matter of defacing public property." Chad gestured toward one of the more colorfully chalked concrete squares. "Who's going to clean *that* up?"

164

"In short," said the mayor, "we need to shut this down, Officer. We need to shut it down immediately." His left eye twitched as he white-knuckled his nubby steering wheel. "Before I get another call from Chauncy Chiltington or James Willoughby or anybody else threatening to have me removed from office!"

"Rules are rules," said Chad. "You break them, you pay the price."

That's when Luigi's mother came trundling down the steps of the front stoop. "Luigi? What's going on?"

"He's up to his usual antics, Momma," said Mary. "Dreaming up foolish games. Bringing disgrace to our family."

"Well said, young lady," said Jimmy.

"Well said indeed," added Chiltington.

"Clean this up, kids," said the cop, climbing back into his car. "Now."

The police car drove away.

The mayor drove away.

Chiltington and Willoughby pedaled their bikes up the street. They were laughing and snickering the whole way.

"Jerks," muttered Bruno, but he seemed to have lost all his fight.

Luigi handed out refunds to all the contestants who never got a chance to take a trip around the board. A lot of neighbors walked away shaking their heads.

Maggie and Chester took down the big spinner. All of Luigi's brothers and sisters drifted off, probably hoping nobody would realize that they were related to the kid named Lemoncello, the one in the clownish clothes and hat.

Luigi sank down to the curb and held his head in his hands. This was worse than the indoor game with the golf ball and the slingshot.

Mary was right.

He had, once again, embarrassed his family.

This time in front of the whole neighborhood.

"Ever think you'll try this sidewalk board-game idea again?" asked Bruno after they finished cleaning up.

"Maybe," said Luigi. "But not here. Not in Ohio."

"Chiltington and Willoughby set you up," said Maggie. "It was payback for the other night at the carnival."

"They're such spoiled brats," said Chester. "They think they own this whole town."

"Yeah," said Bruno. "Probably because they do."

Luigi had already divvied up the money they earned before the game was shut down. After awarding prizes to the winners, he and his three friends pocketed nine dollars each. They would've made more if Chiltington and Willoughby hadn't sabotaged them.

"Buck up, me bucko," said Professor Marvelmous when Luigi reported for work at three p.m. "We all make mistakes. Why, I've learned so much from my mistakes, I'm eager to make a few more."

"But my mother is upset."

"Why? Because you were ambitious and showed gumption, not to mention ingenuity? Pishposh. From the way you tell the tale, and from what I heard from my keenly observant niece, it isn't that your mother is mad at you, but rather that your sister Mary is jealous of you."

"Mary? Why should she be jealous of me?"

"Because, Luigi, you have found your true calling and are now developing the skills to go along with it. She, unfortunately, has not yet found her spark. The thing that makes her who she is and who she shall be. I'm afraid Mary, like so many, is still struggling to learn what it is that makes her shine. What gift she has been given that she might share with the world."

"She'd make a great tattletale or blabbermouth," muttered Luigi.

"Tut-tut," said Professor Marvelmous, wagging his finger at Luigi. "We must have compassion for those who have not yet journeyed as far as we have along this twisty, turny path we call life, which was twisty and turny long before the Milton Bradley board game of the same name."

Luigi nodded. And when he did, he noticed that the knees of the professor's pants were dirty.

"Um, sir?" said Luigi. "You might want to brush that mud off your trousers."

Professor Marvelmous looked down and saw the caked dirt.

"Oh my. I had not noticed that. Thank you, Luigi. Earlier today, whilst you and your chums were hosting your sidewalk board game, I did a little gardening. Planting seeds for a glorious future. Because to plant a garden is to believe that tomorrow will be bright and sunny. Or rainy. You need a little bit of both for blossoms to bloom."

"I'm not so sure about the future being glorious," said Luigi. "And forget the sun. All I ever get is rain."

"Oh, now you're just moping. Boo-hoo-hoo. Boo-hoo-dee-hoo-dee-hoo." And then he blew his nose so loudly, it sounded like a cow passing gas.

Luigi had to laugh.

"The game is never over until it's over," said the professor. "If you get a 'go back three spaces' card in Monopoly, do you quit?"

"No, sir."

"Of course you don't. You take the setback, and when it's next your turn, you pick up the dice, you roll again, and you press onward. You just need a new idea, Luigi. Something to make everybody forget about today's unfortunate unpleasantness."

"You're right," said Luigi. "I just need to think up something bigger. Something wackier. Something even more me!"

That Saturday the booth got so busy that Professor Marvelmous kept it open until ten-thirty.

"It's our last weekend here in Alexandriaville," the professor reminded Luigi. "Monday will be closing night. Therefore, we must make hay while the sun shines and we have the proper hay-making machinery!"

Luigi came home very late, but his parents were waiting for him.

"Luigi?" said his mother.

"Yes?"

"Your father and I need to talk to you."

Here it comes, thought Luigi. He slumped his shoulders and lowered his eyes.

But instead of scolding him, his mother said, "We are both so very proud of you."

"Your hard work will take you far, Luigi," said Mr. Lemoncello. "You have so many fun and clever ideas. And your friend Chester? That boy has a brilliant future ahead of him too!"

Luigi looked up in surprise. "You guys aren't mad about this morning?"

"Ha!" said his mother. "It might've been a good thing. Now Mayor Hannigan knows how many potholes we have on Poplar Lane."

"*And* how many broken streetlights!" added Luigi's father.

On Sunday morning, before the Lemoncello family went to church, Maggie called with that day's puzzle-box report.

"Another stuffed animal. A rhinoceros."

"Huh," said Luigi.

Yeah. The puzzle box had sort of lost its razzle-dazzle.

At church, Luigi went through the motions of the mass—kneeling, standing, and sitting when he was supposed to. But the whole time he was thinking. Thinking. Thinking, thinking, thinking. He needed a new idea. Some kind of incredible new game. It didn't need to be a moneymaker. Just something to make everybody forget his flops and failures.

He kept trying to think during Sunday-afternoon dinner.

Think, think, think.

But the dining room was too noisy. No way could Luigi think amazing new thoughts trapped inside that kind of chaos.

After dinner, he went down to the front stoop of the brownstone, where the only sound came from car tires humming along somewhere in the distance.

He found a bent nail that must have been pried out of the Spin-o-matic's support beams. He used it to scratch a coded message into one of the wrought-iron railings running along the side of the steps:

!KNIHT FLESYM RAEH OT DEEN I

It was a simple code. Slightly more complicated than the childish First Letters game.

This time, all he did was write his message backward:

I NEED TO HEAR MYSELF THINK!

Because he needed to come up with a new, bigger, bolder idea.

Some kind of fantabulous game where the Chiltingtons and Willoughbys weren't the ones writing the rules.

Most of Sunday night was a blur at the carnival.

Luigi kept the balloons pumped and the puzzles scrolling, but his mind drifted away from the fairgrounds.

What kind of new game could he create?

"It's splenderrific to daydream, Luigi," said Professor Marvelmous. "But might I suggest that you not do it in front of the balloon board? We don't want you to be injured by an errant dart. The world needs your genius, not to mention your torso, unpunctured by pointy-tipped projectiles."

"You really think I'm a genius?" said Luigi.

"All children are born geniuses," said the professor. "The hard part is staying one once you grow up."

The next morning was Monday. The final day for the carnival. Luigi wanted to bounce his new game idea off the professor before he moved to the next town. But first he had to come up with one. He headed back to his favorite place to think: the library. Chester and Bruno were with him. Fusilli tagged along too.

"Hi, guys," said Maggie, who was already standing on the library's front porch when they arrived. She held up that morning's prize—a tiny gray elephant on a key chain. "The tenth door opened. The puzzle box is now, officially, history!"

"Did the clockworks inside stop ticking?" asked Chester.

Maggie nodded. "Yep. It ran out of gas. It's just a big empty wooden box again."

"Seems like a lot of work to deliver stuffed animal dolls and a few coins," said Bruno.

"It was fun," said Maggie, with a shrug.

Bruno rolled his eyes. "If you say so. Now, if every door had a thousand bucks hidden behind it, that would've been totally cool!"

Fusilli trotted off to nap in the shade of his oak tree. Mrs. Tobin helped Chester find a back issue of *Popular Mechanics* magazine.

"I need to work out one last glitch on the Pump 'N' Pedal bike," he told Luigi.

Maggie picked up *From the Mixed-Up Files of Mrs. Basil E. Frankweiler,* because Chester had recommended it.

Bruno was happy with the air-conditioning and flipping through a baseball magazine.

"Are you gonna check out a book, Luigi?" asked Maggie.

"Nah. I'm just going to find a quiet corner and think up a new idea for a game."

"You know that's not how you get an idea, right?"

"What do you mean?"

"You don't sit in a corner and say, 'Oooh, I need to think up an idea!' That's not how it works. That's why they call it an 'aha' moment. Ideas sneak up and surprise you!"

"Well, I'm kind of in a hurry, Maggie. This is my last night at the carnival. After tonight, I won't be anything special. I'll just be Lemoncello kid number six again."

"Suit yourself."

Maggie sat down in a comfy chair and started reading her book. Bruno and Chester both settled in with their magazines.

Luigi went into the next room, which was empty, and took a sunny seat at a table near a window.

He pulled out his spiral notebook, uncapped his ballpoint pen, and began to think.

And doodle.

And think some more.

"Whatcha doin'?" whispered a soft voice that knocked Luigi out of his thoughts. It was Vinny.

"Thinking up a new game."

"For here in the library?"

"Maybe," said Luigi. "And Vinny?"

"Yeah?"

"I have great expectations for you. Why, even in hard times, I'll bet you'd be singing a Christmas carol!"

Vinny was confused.

Until, in a flash, he wasn't!

He raced out of the room and came back lugging a stack of three books by Charles Dickens—*Great Expectations, Hard Times,* and *A Christmas Carol.*

Aha, thought Luigi. *I might've just invented a new game!*

A book-title scavenger hunt.

Bruno, Chester, and Maggie ambled into the room. Luigi glanced up at the wall clock. It was nearly twelve.

"Here they come," he said. "The noonday friends."

Vinny was off like a shot to track down another book.

"Where's he going?" asked Maggie.

"I think I just invented a game without even trying to invent one. A library scavenger hunt. I use a book title in a sentence. The players have to figure out what it is they're searching for *and* go find it!"

Vinny was panting when he came back with *The Noonday Friends* by Mary Stolz.

"Well done, Vinny. You're the winner of today's game."

Maggie pulled out her pocket watch. "Speaking of games, it's almost twelve. Almost time for today's radio riddle."

Luigi laughed. "I think I've created a game-playing monster."

"It's fun!"

"You guys go ahead," said Chester. "I've already won once. Besides, I figured out how to fix that bicycle glitch!"

"And, like I told you guys before," said Bruno, "I'm not really into the whole radio contest thing."

"Are you sure?" said Maggie. "Because Luigi and I already won, so we can't play either."

Bruno shrugged. "Sorry. Not interested."

"Okay. But they already announced today's prize. It's a good one."

Bruno faked a yawn to show Maggie how bored he was.

"It's really too bad you're not interested, Bruno," she said. "Because, guess what? They're giving away a year's worth of movie tickets. For two!"

Bruno's eyes went wide.

"What do I have to do to win?"

"And that's Jerry Butler moving up ten spots on the charts, all the way to number twenty!"

Luigi, Bruno, Maggie, and Fusilli were sitting in the shade outside the library, listening to *The Dave Ray-D-O Show* on WALX.

"And, as promised, here comes what has to be the number one prize of the summer," the deejay jabbered. "A whole year's worth of free movie passes for you and a guest. That's going out to the first WALX-keteer to find today's hidden treasure!"

QUACK, QUACK!

"Here's your clue: 'Don't overthink it. You're looking for a trinket.' "

"Oui, oui," said a second, even smoother radio voice.

"That's my newsman, Brian Britain. He's been eating too many French fries. Hey, speaking of France, let's all get up and dance like we have ants in our pants. . . ."

A tune with a funky dance beat started up. Bruno reached over and snapped off the radio.

"We need to head downtown," he said.

"Where to?" asked Luigi.

"The Bijou Theater, where your pops works."

"How'd you get that?" asked Maggie.

"Easy. 'Bijou' is a French word. That's why Dave Ray and the news guy were doing all that French stuff at the end. 'Bijou' means 'jewel' or 'trinket.' "

"And you know all this because . . . ?" asked Maggie.

"My dad served in France. The Seventieth Tank Battalion. He told me what 'bijou' meant one time when we were at the movies. Come on."

Fusilli barked, and they took off running.

Two minutes later they were on Main Street.

"There!" said Maggie. "Taped to the movie theater's ticket-booth window!"

The Willoughby Bijou was closed on Monday afternoons, but there was a bright blue WALX note card stuck to the glass just below the small slatted circle the ticket seller talked through.

TAKE ME DOWN THE STREET
TO CLAIM YOUR PRIZE.
PEACE AND LOVE,
THE WALX GUYS

"All right!" shouted Bruno, tearing the card off the glass. "I did it. I can't believe I actually won. And I got the top prize of the summer too! Yes!"

He gave himself a triumphant arm pump.

Luigi was happy to see his friend acting like his old self again.

"The radio station is just down the block," said Maggie. "At the corner of Main and Elm."

The three friends ran down the block with Fusilli wagging his tail behind them.

"Wait here!" Luigi told his dog when they reached a glass door with a WALX decal plastered on it.

Fusilli sat down. He would wait.

Bruno, Luigi, and Maggie practically yanked the door off its hinges as they bounded into the building and climbed up a steep set of steps to the second floor.

They could still hear the thumping dance tune. It was playing on a radio sitting on the receptionist's desk.

"Can I help you kids?" the lady behind the desk asked. Her hair looked like a blond beehive.

"Yes, ma'am!" said Bruno, holding up the blue card. "My name is Bruno Depinna, and I won today's contest."

"Uh-huh. Just a minute."

The receptionist picked up her phone and punched a blinking button.

"Dave? I have a Bruno Depinna here. Yes, he solved it that quick." She winked at Bruno. "Uh-huh. Okay."

She hung up the phone.

"Head down the hall to where you see that red blinking light. That means Dave's on the air, so whatever you do, don't open the door or make any noise until he calls you into the studio. Got it?"

"Yes, ma'am," said Bruno.

The three friends made their way down the hall to a big window. A long-haired man in tinted aviator glasses was dancing in front of a console filled with all sorts of big knobs and bouncing meters. It had to be Dave Ray. He grabbed the accordion arm holding his foam-topped microphone and pulled it closer to his mouth.

He also punched a blinking square button and, all of a sudden, a horse whinnied and neighed.

"Hi-ho, Silver. I'm up on my feet and dancing to the beat. That's 'The Horse' on WALX. Stick around, because we already have a winner for today's treasure hunt. But first we need to pay some bills."

The disc jockey slid a tape cartridge into a player and bopped its blinking button.

"Let's All Go See a Will-ough-by," sang a chorus of jingle singers, "Let's All Go See a Will-ough-by."

A mellow announcer with a very deep voice took over. "Yes, let's all go see the finest in cinematic excellence playing at the Willoughby Bijou Theater. Located on Main Street in . . ."

The deejay twisted one of the big black knobs in front of him. The commercial's sound faded away. He turned to the window and gestured for everybody to come on in.

Bruno pulled open the soundproof door. Luigi and Maggie followed him into the broadcast booth.

"Hey, kids. I'm Dave Ray. Darlene out front tells me we have a winner?"

"Yes, sir," said Bruno, holding up the blue card.

"Far out. When we come out of the commercial, we'll do something live. Cool?"

"Cool," said Bruno.

Luigi felt a whoosh of air as someone else opened the broadcast booth behind them.

"Excuse me, Mr. Ray."

Luigi spun around.

It was Jimmy Willoughby.

"Oh, hey, Jimbo," said the disc jockey. "What's up?"

"This . . . *listener* . . . can't win my father's prize."

"Why not?" protested Bruno.

"What's the problemo?" asked the deejay. "Lay it on me, man."

Dave Ray seemed nervous, like somehow Jimmy Willoughby scared him.

"He's trying to cheat. To trick my father's radio station into awarding him a prize he hasn't actually earned."

Maggie's mouth dropped open. "Wait a second. Your father owns this radio station?"

Jimmy smirked. "Indeed he does."

"That's how we have this amaze-a-mundo prize today," said Dave Ray. "They call it cross-promotion. Willoughby movie theater, Willoughby radio station. I just call it groovy."

"But I won," Bruno insisted.

"He peeled the blue card off the movie-theater box office window before anyone else," Luigi told the disc jockey.

Jimmy shook his head. "We weren't looking for a blue card, were we, Mr. Ray?"

"I dunno, man . . ."

"Check your log. There. On the clipboard."

The disc jockey picked up a clipboard with a schedule grid filled with notes.

"Bummer. Says here the winner will have a *golden* note card."

"Like this one," said Chad Chiltington, strolling into the crowded booth and flipping and flapping a golden card.

Willoughby turned to Maggie. "We've observed how interested you've been in playing all our radio games."

"That's why you've been shadowing us?" said Luigi.

"Yes. My father and I feared that you troublemakers would stoop to cheating someday."

"I didn't cheat," said Bruno.

"Neither did I!" insisted Maggie.

"None of us cheated!" added Luigi.

"Your word against ours," said Willoughby. "And let me remind you, those who give out the prizes always get to choose who receives them."

"If you ever tell me 'games are fair' again, Luigi, I'm gonna punch you in the nose!"

Bruno was fuming as the three friends and Fusilli marched up Main Street. He kicked at every pebble and chunk of rock that dared cross his path.

"Those two preppies are the ones who cheated!" said Maggie.

Fusilli barked in agreement.

Luigi shook his head. "I can't believe Mr. Willoughby owns the radio station, too."

"He owns this whole stupid town!" said Bruno. "Willoughby gave Chiltington that golden card before the game even got started. There was no way to win unless you were already one of the winners. Unless your old man owns the radio station and the movie theater and everything else. . . ."

Bruno was muttering.

Maggie was mad.

Fusilli was growling.

And all Luigi could do was think about how he wanted to stop the Chiltingtons and Willoughbys of the world from ruining everybody else's fun.

That evening at the balloon booth, Luigi told Professor Marvelmous what had happened at the radio station.

"It was so unfair."

"Well, hopefully, as a young man much wiser than me once said, 'the times they are a-changin'.' Fun shouldn't just belong to the people with power. We're all counting on you, Luigi, to change that. To change this world for the better."

"But I'm only thirteen."

"Then what are you waiting for? There's no time like the present."

This was the last night of the summer carnival. Luigi's last night to learn from his teacher, Professor Marvelmous.

"Tomorrow I move on to Bowling Green, Ohio," the professor told him. "I'm not sure if that means that they have an outdoor bowling alley or a golf course where everybody putts with bowling balls. Suffice it to say, I'm eager to find out."

Before Marvelmous took his late-afternoon hot-tea-with-honey break to soothe his raw throat, he rattled some coins out of the Band-Aid box.

"Need fifteen cents to purchase the tea . . ."

Something caught his eye. "Oh my. A 1964 quarter. That's a keeper."

"You're a coin collector, right?" said Luigi.

"I prefer the term 'numismatist.' It sounds so much more mysterious. I'm hoping Maggie will, one day, pick up the hobby."

"Is that why there were five pennies in the puzzle box?"

The professor giggled a little—like he'd just told himself a secret joke. "I suppose that's one explanation."

"Is there another?"

"Hard to say. But there usually is. Toodle-oo."

Professor Marvelmous pocketed the quarter along with three nickels and headed off to the Buckeye Diner. Luigi was confused by that last remark.

Was there another explanation? Why the five pennies?

Unfortunately, he didn't have time to puzzle over it. He popped on his top hat and stepped in as the booth barker.

He saw Vinny from the library in the crowd. There was a lady with short black hair standing next to him. Luigi wondered if she was Vinny's mom.

Luigi gave Vinny his own personalized spiel. He also scrolled the puzzles forward to one he was sure Vinny would love.

"Step right up to my phantom tollbooth. This is where the wild things are. Me? I'm the giving tree!"

Vinny edged forward. The lady followed after him. A hint of a smile blossomed on her face.

"Hello, young man," said Luigi, tipping his top hat. "Would you like to play?"

Vinny nodded and carefully placed a quarter on the table.

Luigi handed him five darts.

The kid was pretty good. His five throws popped five balloons and revealed some hair, the word "the," a purring cat, and a box of crayons.

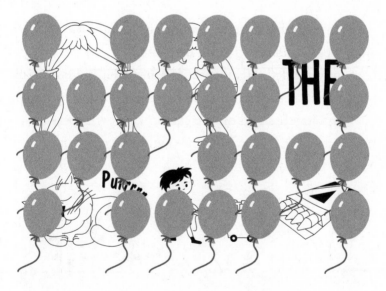

"Would you like to solve the puzzle?" Luigi asked.

Vinny shook his head and plunked down another quarter on the plywood plank.

Then he tossed five more darts and cleared five more balloons.

187

"Oh my, what excellent shooting," said Luigi. "Eat too many beans and you'll wind up tooting."

Vinny giggled. His mother laughed. But his smile vanished when he realized that a crowd had started forming.

"Just stay focused on the game," Luigi whispered.

Vinny took a deep breath, bought five more darts, and popped five more balloons.

"Oh!" cried Luigi. "Fantabulous! For any prize in the booth, can you solve this puzzle?"

Vinny nodded.

But he didn't say anything.

"Go on, kid," urged one of the spectators.

Vinny looked squeamish. Sick, even. Like maybe he'd eaten too much carnival food.

"Come on, pal," said a man. "Other people wanna play!"

Luigi knew that Vinny didn't like talking in public. So he improvised.

"What's that? You're so confident you know the answer you want to write it down? Very well. I accept your bold and audacious—dare I say, boldacious—challenge!"

Luigi dug a spiral flip pad and pen out of the back pocket of his jeans. He handed them to Vinny.

Vinny scribbled down the answer. He closed the notepad and handed it back to Luigi.

Luigi made a big show of carefully, cautiously, slowly peeling open the pad.

And then he gasped.

"*Harold and the Purple Crayon?*" said Luigi.

He whipped around and brandished the nail-on-a-pole tool he used to pick up trash around the booth. He popped the rest of the balloons with its tip and tapped each image in the rebus puzzle.

"Hair. Old. And. The. Purr. Pull. Crayon. Huzzah! You are correct!"

The crowd cheered and applauded. Vinny's mother clapped the loudest. She was misty-eyed when she said, "Thank you," to Luigi. Vinny and his mom went home with a big plastic piggy bank and even bigger smiles.

Professor Marvelmous stepped into the booth. He'd seen the whole thing.

"Well done, me bucko. Keep striving to do things for other people. Not because of who they are or what they might do in return. Do it because of who *you* are!"

"Let's not say goodbye," Professor Marvelmous proclaimed to the sparse crowd that gathered on the fairgrounds the next morning to bid him farewell. "Let us simply say, 'See you next summer!' And if you're itching for another balloon to pop, be sure to go to your next birthday party with a safety pin."

The crowd laughed and clapped.

About an hour later, when his trailer was closed up tight and hitched to the back of his pickup truck, Professor Marvelmous handed the wooden puzzle box to Maggie.

"You should keep this," he said. "You earned it."

"Is it okay if I let Luigi and Chester play with it?" she asked. "They probably want to figure out how it works."

"Of course, of course. Just don't let anybody attack it with a sledgehammer."

Luigi laughed.

"I'm gonna put this in Mom's car," said Maggie, carrying the puzzle box across the field to where her mother had parked the family station wagon.

"Professor?" said Luigi when Maggie was far enough away.

"Yes, Luigi?"

"First of all—thank you. For everything. I owe you so much."

"You do?" The professor gasped. "Were you pilfering coins from my money box?"

"No, sir. I'd never—"

"I know, Luigi. I was joshing. You are the best apprentice I've ever had."

"Um, I think I'm also the only apprentice you've ever had."

"Oh, were I to have five thousand more, none would be as Luigi-ish as you!"

Luigi smiled. "Can I ask you something?"

"Certainly. Ask away!"

"Okay," said Luigi, taking a deep breath. "I'm thinking about putting together a treasure hunt. Something bigger and better than what Mr. Willoughby's radio station does."

The professor nodded. "Treasure hunts can be sublime. Just make sure your clues always rhyme. And also be certain that everyone has a fair shot at winning if their brains they use to unravel those rhyming clues."

"Got it," said Luigi.

Maggie came back to say her final goodbyes.

"It was great to see you again, Uncle Clarence."

"It was marvelmous seeing you, Maggie," said the professor, giving her a hug. "And I am so pleased with your progress."

"Progress? What do you mean?"

"Why, you've come so far. You've learned so much. Spending time with young Mr. Lemoncello and his friends has been stupendously good for you. It might even prove to be the key to your future!"

"I, uh, guess . . ."

"I sense that you are now ready!"

"For what?"

"For whatever mysterious surprises life may bring your way. Happiness often sneaks in through a door you did not know was open. Adieu! Adieu! I hope to see you again on Thanksgiving, Margaret, and, in the meantime, I will say several silent prayers that your mother, my sister, forgets how to make that Jell-O mold with the pineapple chunks buried inside it." He shivered as if he'd just had a horrible nightmare. "Oooh. The horror, the horror. Toodle-oo!"

Luigi and Maggie waved as the professor climbed into the cab of his truck, cranked up the engine, and lurched away, dragging the booth behind him.

Luigi sighed. "I'm gonna miss him."

"Yeah," said Maggie. "Me too."

"I figured out what was wrong with the bike," said Chester.

"That's great!" said Luigi. He and his two best friends were back in their alley, examining Professor Marvelmous's wooden puzzle box.

"It was in the transfer clutch that shifts power from the pedals to the handlebars," Chester chattered excitedly. "Now it rides like a dream! It's speedy, too! How are you doing with the puzzle box?"

Luigi shook his head. "Still a puzzle."

"You want me to go grab a sledgehammer out of the toolshed?" asked Bruno, poking at the box with a stick.

"No," said Luigi. "I promised Professor Marvelmous we wouldn't smash this thing to pieces."

"Why'd you promise him something dumb like that?"

"Because this is a work of art."

"Says you."

"Says everybody who's ever seen it."

"Not me," Bruno huffed.

"Fine," said Luigi. "I'll take it upstairs. Figure out how it works myself."

"Fine. You do that."

"I will."

"See if I care."

"You're still mad, aren't you?" Chester said to Bruno. "About getting ripped off at the radio station."

"Maybe," said Bruno.

Luigi couldn't blame Bruno for being upset. Fun shouldn't just belong to a handful of powerful people who could snatch it away from everybody else. Like the professor said, no matter the game, you had to make sure that everybody who played had a fair shot at winning.

"So how about we get back at them?" said Luigi.

"What?"

"Who says the radio station is the only one in town that can do a treasure hunt?" said Luigi. "It's time someone gave WALX a little friendly competition."

Bruno snorted. "Who? You?"

"No, Bruno," said Luigi. "*Us.*"

"Fun for all and all for fun," said Chester, raising his invisible sword.

Bruno gave him a withering look. Chester lowered his arm.

"I've figured out how we could do it," said Luigi. "I've got it all mapped out up here." He tapped the side of his head.

Bruno rolled his eyes.

Luigi kept going. "First, Bruno, like you always say, we need a really cool prize."

"Like what?" said Bruno dismissively. "An autographed copy of your First Letters card game?"

"No. Not that."

"I've got an idea," said Chester. "Maybe the winner could get a free ride on the Pump 'N' Pedal."

Now Bruno rolled his eyes up to the sky. "Bad idea."

"No it's not. We go around town, selling clues and treasure maps," said Luigi. "Of course, like Professor Marvelmous told me, all the clues will have to rhyme."

"Of course," said Chester.

"We hide a treasure chest someplace cool," added Luigi. "Like in the fountain in front of the Parker House hotel."

"It'll have to be an insulated treasure chest," said Chester. "Waterproof."

"And this is going to defeat the WALX treasure hunts?" said Bruno. "Hiding an insulated treasure chest underwater in a grungy fountain filled with slimy algae so people can ride around on a bike that'll make them look like a nork?" He did his ridiculously exaggerated arm gestures again. "Meanwhile, Mr. Willoughby and his cronies are on the radio yakking about their clues and their awesome prizes and we're running around town, knocking on doors, reciting rhymes?" He shook his head. "I'm so sick of both of you!"

Bruno's sudden anger stunned Luigi.

"Count me out," he fumed. "It's a waste of time. You guys are a waste of time. And, by the way, how come we never do anything I want to do?"

"Okay," said Luigi. "What do you want to do?"

"I want to be one of the winners! That's who I want to hang out with, too. The guys with all the prizes. You know, Luigi, your sister Mary's right. You need to get your head out of the clouds, man. Down here on earth, the Willoughbys and the Chiltingtons are in charge. We're just pawns in *their* game. Remember, 'those who give out the prizes always get to choose who receives them.'"

"B-b-but—"

"Save it. I'm out of here."

"Where are you going?" asked Chester, sounding hurt.

"I dunno. But I know I like the prizes more than the game. So maybe I'll just try to find a summer job. Make some money like you did, Luigi. Maybe Mr. Willoughby needs somebody to shine his shoes. After all, he's the only real game in town."

Bruno stomped up the alley.

"What about the three musketeers?" Chester called after him.

"Give my spot to somebody else," hollered Bruno without even turning around. "Maybe Maggie. You two like her and her dorky hats so much. . . ."

"Bruno?" shouted Luigi. "Wait a second!"

Bruno spun around and practically spat out his words.

"And don't you ever come by my place to watch *Concentration* again either. I hate that stupid show! I hate all your stupid games!"

And with that, Bruno was gone.

Maybe for good, thought Luigi.

"He's just super upset," said Chester, digging his toe into the crackled asphalt.

"Yeah. So, you still want to do the treasure hunt?"

Chester shrugged. "Maybe. I don't know. I want to test-drive the Pump 'N' Pedal some more first."

"Sure." Luigi gestured to the puzzle box. "Mind if I take this upstairs?"

"I don't care," said Chester. "See you later, Luigi."

"Yeah," said Luigi. "Later."

And he hauled the heavy wooden box up four flights to his apartment.

For the first time in over a week, Luigi was still home at three o'clock in the afternoon.

The summer carnival was gone. Done. Finished.

He pulled back a curtain and peered down into the alley. Chester was there, tinkering with the bike he and Luigi's father had been working on. It had a long, curved banana seat and high-rise handlebars. It was painted candy-apple red and had shiny chrome fenders over the knobby front and rear tires.

It looked awesome.

Luigi grabbed the sketch of a treasure-chest idea he'd been doodling on for the past few hours and raced down the staircase to the building's rear entrance.

"That's so cool!" he gushed as he entered the alleyway.

"Thanks," said Chester. "Your dad's down in the

basement, scrounging around for one last piece of hardware we could use to make it even faster." Chester saw the sheet of graph paper in Luigi's hand. "What's that?"

"I've been working on a design for a puzzle-box treasure chest."

"So when you find the box, you still have to solve another riddle to actually get to the treasure?"

"Exactly! I was thinking we could use a combination lock. One of those ones with letters. But I need your help, Chester. I'm good at dreaming things up. You're good at actually making them."

Chester wiped his hands clean on his jeans. "Let me take a closer look at that treasure chest."

"This treasure hunt will be so much better than the one on WALX!" said Luigi. "Does the radio station have a puzzle box? No, they do not!"

"So it's true?" said a voice from over where the alley met the street. "You two thieves are stealing our radio station's treasure-hunt idea?"

It was Jimmy Willoughby. Chad Chiltington was right beside him.

So was Bruno.

"Well done, Bruno," said Chiltington. "Thank you for coming to us with this information. This town needs more upstanding young citizens like you."

Bruno dropped his eyes. It was like he couldn't even look at Luigi or Chester.

"Bruno?" Luigi could barely say his friend's name. "What'd you do?"

"His duty," said Willoughby. "He told us what you two were plotting."

Chiltington shook his head. "Theft of intellectual property is against all the rules."

"I did what I had to do, okay, Luigi?" Bruno blurted. He was trying to act tough, but it sounded more like he wanted to burst into tears.

He backed up a step or two.

"I gotta go. I'm late for work."

"Work?" asked Chester.

"That's right! I'm making money. Just like you used to make, Luigi."

With that, he turned on his heel and ran away.

"Mr. Depinna found a summer job," said Jimmy. "He's the newest dishwasher at my father's Buckeye Diner."

Man, thought Luigi, *Bruno was right. The Willoughbys do own everything in this town—even the diner.*

Just then, a long black car eased to a stop on the street. The driver, a man wearing a dark suit and a chauffeur's cap, hurried around the front of the vehicle to open the rear passenger-side door.

A tall, lanky man stepped out. The man had snowy-white hair, a stern expression, and the nose of an eagle. He carried himself as if he were an English lord.

"Are these the two boys, James?" he inquired.

"Yes, Father."

Luigi gulped. The kingly man was Mr. Willoughby.

"Which one of you dreamed up this sidewalk board game James and Chadwick told me about?"

Luigi very tentatively raised his hand.

"His name is Luigi Lemoncello," said Chiltington.

"That's why nobody was at the early movie on Saturday," said Jimmy. "And why nobody was shopping at the store, either. And now these two juvenile delinquents want to do their own treasure hunt."

"They stole that idea from your radio station, sir," added Chiltington.

Mr. Willoughby moved closer to Luigi. With every step he took, Luigi could hear the leather crinkling in his shiny shoes. The man examined Luigi the way he might inspect an underdone baked potato sitting beside his prime rib.

"You have a lot of big ideas, eh, boy?"

"W-w-well . . . ," Luigi stammered.

If this were a book or a movie, Luigi thought, *this is when Mr. Willoughby would surprise everybody and say, "Well done, lad! Hard work and ingenuity like yours should be rewarded! I want you and your big ideas working for me! And I want to give your father a raise too!"*

But this wasn't a book or a movie.

"Is your father, by any chance, Angelo Lemoncello?"

Luigi didn't answer.

He didn't have to.

His dad came up out of the apartment building's basement. He was staring down at a greasy piece of hardware in his hand.

"Chester, I think this flange should do the trick. We'll need to—"

He looked up and saw his boss. "Mr. Willoughby. Good afternoon, sir."

"Is this your son?" Mr. Willoughby nodded, ever so slightly, toward Luigi.

"Yes. That's Luigi. He's a very clever boy."

"You should keep your 'very clever boy' on a tighter leash. That sidewalk board game he hosted last weekend hurt ticket sales at the Bijou. Now he's planning a town-wide treasure hunt in direct competition with those being run by my radio station."

"Well," said Luigi's father, "I'm sure—"

Mr. Willoughby showed Luigi's father the palm of his hand.

"Save your breath, Angelo. I am not interested. I am also no longer interested in your projectionist services at my movie theater. Especially since it has been brought to my attention that you snuck your son into my auditorium for free!"

Mr. Lemoncello's shoulders sagged. He knew that charge was true. Except he hadn't just snuck in Luigi. He'd snuck in all ten Lemoncello kids.

"I also think it's high time *my* son, James, learned the

family business. I'm going to start him out at the bottom. I'm giving him your job at my department store."

"Ha!" laughed Chiltington. "You have to work!"

"Chadwick?" fumed Mr. Willoughby.

"Sir?"

"Your father has a job lined up for you as well. You start tomorrow."

"Yes, sir."

"So you're firing me, Mr. Willoughby?" said Luigi's dad. "From both jobs?"

For the first time since he stepped into the alleyway, Mr. Willoughby smiled.

"Yes, Angelo. I am."

"You're not to blame," Mr. Lemoncello told Luigi and Chester after both Willoughbys and Chad Chiltington were gone.

"I'm sorry, Poppa," said Luigi.

"Hush. Mr. Willoughby is a warped, frustrated old man. I'll find another job. Don't worry."

He took hold of the bicycle's handlebars. "Chester?"

"Yes, sir?"

"I'm gonna make that last little fix. Then, tomorrow? Get ready to fly!"

Putting on a brave smile, Luigi's dad pushed the shiny bike toward the building superintendent's small workshop at the far end of the alleyway.

"I guess we won't be doing our treasure hunt, huh?" said Chester.

"Guess not." Luigi looked up the alley toward the

street. To where Bruno had betrayed him and Chester. "What happened to Bruno?"

Chester shrugged. "I don't know. Maybe he was thinking too much about prizes and winning instead of just having fun playing the game."

That night at dinner, both tables were eerily quiet.

No one was shouting to be heard. No one was laughing or talking about their day. Even the plates and bowls didn't seem to clatter as loudly as they usually did. They sat silent on their railroad tracks.

"We'll be okay," Luigi's mother assured everyone.

"Of course we will," said Mr. Lemoncello. "Tomorrow is a new day. I'll go out and I'll find a new job. One where I don't have to work for Mr. Willoughby."

When he said that, Tomasso turned to give Luigi a dirty look. Mary tsked her tongue at him. The little ones just seemed worried.

They'd all seen how Luigi had treated Chiltington and Willoughby at the carnival. They all knew he was to blame for what had happened to their father.

They're right, thought Luigi.

He'd wanted a way to stand out from his brothers and sisters. And now, unfortunately, he'd found it.

"Eat your food before it gets cold," said their mother. Luigi knew what this really meant: *Eat now because, thanks to Luigi, we may not have any food this time next week.*

Luigi pushed his food around his plate with his fork. He wasn't hungry.

"Do you want to play a game?" Sofia whispered from across the table. "We could play your spelling game with the cards."

Luigi shook his head.

He was done with games.

The next morning, Luigi didn't want to go to the library with Chester.

"Why not?" asked Chester. "Mrs. Tobin might know a good book to cheer you up."

"I don't want to read a 'good book,'" said Luigi. "Most stories have sappy happy endings where the good guys win. Bruno was right. Life isn't a game. There are no rules to make everything fair and square. The Chiltingtons and Willoughbys cheat, and they always win."

Chester looked at Luigi and shook his head. "Well, of course the bad guys always win if the good guys all throw up their hands and quit. See you later."

Luigi watched his friend walk away.

He went to the bedroom he shared with his brothers, none of whom were speaking to him. Luigi raised the window an inch or two to let in a cooling breeze.

In the afternoon, while Luigi was lying on his bed, seeing nothing but the slats of the bunk above him, Sofia knocked on the bedroom door. "Luigi? I need your help."

"With what?"

"I'm gonna send Massimo a secret message! But since you won't play First Letters with me, I have to make up my own secret code."

"Hang on," said Luigi. He reached under his mattress and pulled out the manila envelope with all the picture cards stuffed inside it. "You can have this."

Sofia's eyes brightened. "Thanks, Luigi!" She ran across the room and gave him a kiss on the cheek. "I still love you, even if everyone else is mad at you."

"And I love you, Sofia."

She skipped out of the room with the cards.

A little before five, Luigi heard the slow clicking and ticking of a bicycle being wheeled across the asphalt alley below. He peeked out the window.

His father was showing Tomasso the finished Pump 'N' Pedal.

"I'm going to roll this over to Chester's. I want him to test-ride it a little more. We made it even speedier."

Tomasso nodded. "Any luck finding a job today?"

Their father shook his head. "No. But tomorrow's always a new day, Tomasso. A new opportunity."

"I'm sorry Luigi ruined our lives, Poppa."

Mr. Lemoncello looked surprised.

"Our lives aren't 'ruined,' Tomasso. I just don't work for Mr. Willoughby anymore. And do you know why?"

"Because Luigi was costing him business and threatening to steal his radio station's treasure-hunt idea. He was also rude to Mr. Willoughby's son at the carnival."

Mr. Lemoncello laughed. "I'm talking about the real reason, Tomasso."

"Real reason?"

"I think Mr. Willoughby is afraid."

"Of what?"

"Luigi."

Now Tomasso had to laugh. "Mr. Willoughby, the richest man in town, is afraid of a thirteen-year-old kid?"

"Oh, yes. Your little brother stole the audience away from the movie theater. He drew the shoppers away from the department store. That's not easy to do, Tomasso. It takes skill. Smarts. And remember—thirteen-year-old kids grow up. When they do, watch out."

"Oh, you can forget about him, Maggie," Luigi heard Chester say down in the alley early the next morning. "Luigi's taken himself off the board. He's hiding in a game box on the top shelf. I think he might stay up in his room for the rest of his life."

"Is he sick?" Maggie asked.

"No. HE'S JUST A BIG BABY!"

Chester had cupped his hands around his mouth to make a megaphone. He was practically screaming because he figured Luigi would be listening. He'd figured right.

"Well," Maggie shouted through *her* cupped hands, "I wish Luigi was down here! I need his help!"

"Oh!" shouted Chester, still aiming his voice up to Luigi's bedroom window. "Do you have a puzzle that you need to solve?"

"Yes!" replied Maggie. "Uncle Clarence sent me a cryptic telegram!"

"You mean it was *strange* and *mysterious*?" said Chester.

Luigi shook his head. Maggie and Chester sounded like bad actors from a bad play who only knew how to read their stilted lines one way: badly.

"Yes, Chester! I need Luigi's help!"

Luigi looked down at his two friends. Neither one was a Willoughby or a Chiltington. They couldn't wave a magic wand and fix everything. They couldn't give his dad a new job.

And whatever "strange and mysterious" puzzle Maggie was struggling with, she'd probably figure it out. Eventually. Like she had with that radio riddle.

But something tugged at the corner of his mind.

He was remembering something Professor Marvelmous had told him on his last day in the booth: *Keep striving to do things for other people, Luigi. Not because of who they are or what they might do in return. Do it because of who you are!*

Who was he?

He smiled.

He was Luigi L. Lemoncello!

He dropped to his knees and dug around under his bed. He'd stuffed his top hat down there when he'd decided to quit being who he was truly meant to be. He put it on and felt the same incredible tingle he'd felt when he wore it in the balloon booth.

He could almost feel the magic, see the bright lights, and hear the roar of the crowd.

It was showtime!

He threw open the bedroom window and stepped out onto the fire escape.

"Fun for all!" he shouted down to his friends.

"And all for fun?" Chester shouted back, looking relieved.

"Luigi?" called Maggie. "What are you doing up there? We need you down here!"

"Never fear, my friends!" he cried. "Luigi L. Lemoncello is on his way!"

He scampered down the fire escape, clunking on the metal steps, pausing at each landing to tip his top hat and say a quick howdy to whoever was inside gawking at him. When he reached the second floor, where the staircase switchbacks ended, he stepped onto the narrow sliding ladder and rode it down to the ground, making sure to extend an arm and a leg so his moves looked more like a ballet.

"Greetings and salutations!" he declared, brandishing his hat in his hand.

Chester shook his head and laughed. "You still know how to make an entrance."

"And *you* know how to throw your voice up four stories!" Luigi turned to Maggie. "What's this about a new puzzle?"

She pulled out a brownish piece of paper with WESTERN UNION printed across the top and sprocket holes down both sides.

"Uncle Clarence sent me a strange telegram."

"Why didn't he just call you on the phone?"

Maggie shrugged. "Because he's Professor Marvelmous?"

Luigi nodded. "Good point."

He read what was typed in the telegram:

```
YOUR QUEST HAS ONLY JUST BEGUN
THE PRIZE WILL BE MORE THAN FUN
PARDON MY PUN
BUT THIS IS THE BIG ONE!
```

"What's it mean?" asked Chester.

"Yeah, Luigi," said Maggie. "A quest is a pretty big deal."

"Like the Knights of the Round Table searching for the Holy Grail," said Chester.

"Or Frodo Baggins's quest in *The Lord of the Rings*," added Maggie.

Luigi rubbed his chin thoughtfully. He wished he had a mustache to fiddle with. "What could be so important that he'd go through all this trouble? Telegrams are expensive...."

"Well, if it's a quest," said Chester, "technically you have to find something and bring it back."

"And it sounds like a gigantic prize," said Luigi.

"But what is it?" said Maggie. "And how do we find it?"

Luigi shook his head. "I have absolutely no idea."

"It could be anything, anywhere," said Chester with a defeated sigh.

"Luigi?" whined a small voice.

Sofia came into the alley. She was pouting.

"What's wrong?" asked Luigi, bending down so they were eye to eye.

"I forget how to make the code."

"Well, what do you want to say?"

"'Look at my doll, Massimo. Isn't she pretty?'"

"Okay. I'll show you how to do the first word. 'Look.' *L-O-O-K*." He reached into the envelope and pulled out the cards he needed. "So, that's llama, orange, orange, kangaroo."

And that's when the penny dropped, the light bulb clicked, and the answer hit.

"Aha!"

"Luigi?" said Sofia. "Why are you staring at me like that?"

"Because you're a genius!"

"I am?"

"Sure. All kids are born geniuses. But you, Sofia, are the smartest one of them all! You just cracked Professor Marvelmous's secret code!"

Until that instant, Luigi had assumed that the puzzle box's daily prizes were just that.

Daily prizes.

Now he realized they might be something more.

"Do you think you can do the rest of the code on your own?" he asked Sofia.

"Nah. I think I'll play with my doll instead of sending Massimo a message. See you later, Luigi."

She scampered back into the apartment building.

Luigi whirled around to face Maggie. "Can you remember the ten prizes in the order you received them?"

"Sure. I mean, I think so."

"What's up, Luigi?" asked Chester.

"I may not be the only one with a first-letters code. Which, by the way, I told your uncle about the night before he gave you the puzzle box. I'm pretty sure Professor

Marvelmous was sending us a message with his ten daily surprises. That's why our 'quest' isn't done yet. They weren't just prizes. They were a code."

Now Chester turned to Maggie. "What was behind each of the ten doors?"

"In the day-by-day order, please," added Luigi. He reached into his jean jacket and found his flip-cover pad and a pen to jot down notes.

Maggie nodded. "Okay. It was a stuffed lion, an owl, an otter, and then a koala. Next came the four pennies and the one penny."

"I remember those," said Chester. "The pennies were an unusual and surprising twist."

"After the coins, I found a meerkat, an ostrich, a rhinoceros, and an elephant."

"Of course!" said Luigi, proudly tapping his pad with the tip of his pen. "*L-O-O-K,* four, one, *M-O-R-E.* Look for one more!"

"One more what?" wondered Chester.

"Another secret compartment!" exclaimed Maggie. "Where's the puzzle box?"

"Up in my room," said Luigi. "I'll go grab it."

Luigi tore into the apartment building and bounded up the four flights of steps in a flash. He practically exploded through the back door of his apartment.

"No running in the house!" Mary shouted at him.

"Sorry."

Luigi ran into his bedroom and scooped up the wooden

puzzle box. Cradling it against his chest, he dashed for the back door.

"Luigi?" shouted Mary, stamping her feet on the kitchen's linoleum floor.

"Great to see you, too, sis. Catch you later!"

He bounded down the steps to the alley.

"Here we go, guys." Luigi positioned the box on top of a lidded garbage can.

"So there's one more secret compartment?" said Maggie, examining the cube closely.

"But where?" said Chester.

He and Luigi ran their fingers along the wooden slats making up the four side panels and top. Nothing budged.

Maggie explored the carved ornaments and doodads. She tried to twist and turn them. Nothing was hinged. Nothing swiveled.

"What about the bottom?" suggested Chester.

They flipped the box over. Chester fidgeted with the four wooden orbs that gave the cube its legs. The third one clicked clockwise.

"I was right! That's how your uncle told the box what day it was."

"But nothing else down here moves," said Maggie.

"We still have the brass keyhole cover up top," said Luigi.

"We used that with one of the wooden rosettes, remember?" said Chester. "Its peg was the key to opening the front panel."

Curiosity contorted Luigi's face. " 'Look for one more,' "

he mumbled. "We only pulled out one rosette on that side," he said aloud. "What if there's another one? What if we look for one more removable peg?"

He flipped the cube around so he was facing the panel with the missing piece in the top right corner. He tried the one in the top left corner. Nothing. He moved down to the bottom right corner. Still nothing. There was only one more remaining: the bottom left corner.

Luigi rubbed his fingertips together the way he'd seen safecrackers do in heist movies.

He pinched the final carved flower between his thumb and forefinger. He gave it a gentle twist to the right.

Bells tinkled and *GLING*ed inside the box.

They heard a whir of gears. The clicking of a slender chain on a sprocket.

The whole back panel of the box slowly lowered to reveal a five-letter combination lock embedded in the lacquered wood above an engraved rebus puzzle:

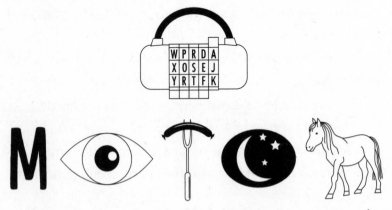

The one more door had led them to one more puzzle.

"Knockwurst!" shouted Chester.

"Excuse me?" said Maggie.

"The third image. You probably think it's a hot dog, but my dad loves to grill sausages, and that's a knockwurst! See how it curves at the tips?"

"The first word is easy," said Luigi. "That's an *M* and an eye, or 'my.' "

"My knockwurst moon horse?" said Maggie.

"The moon's surrounded by stars," said Luigi. "So maybe that's a night sky."

"And that horse could be a mare," said Chester.

The three friends' eyes went wide as they all solved the puzzle at the exact same second.

"My worst nightmare!" they said simultaneously.

"I'm guessing your uncle Clarence's worst nightmare is a five-letter word," said Luigi.

"Snake!" shouted Chester.

"Roach!" tried Luigi.

Maggie grinned and shook her head. "Nope. Uncle Clarence wanted the answer to be something only he and I would know. A family secret we share."

"What is it?" asked Chester.

Maggie looked around like she wanted to make sure no one was eavesdropping. Then she said, "We both hate my mother's Thanksgiving dinner Jell-O mold."

Luigi rolled the letters on the combination lock to J-E-L-L-O.

There was a soft click.

The framed puzzle swung open like a door to reveal a rectangular compartment.

"Looks like Uncle Clarence left me a note," said Maggie as she pulled out an envelope.

"It's another puzzle," she announced, removing a purple card from the envelope. "It's a poem." She showed Chester and Luigi the card:

In the land of fried dough
There is a certain Johnny Pump I do know.
Three feet in front of his face
Lies another Professor Plum for this race.

"The land of fried dough?" said Chester. "I believe that started up in Canada."

"You're thinking of poutine," said Maggie. "French fries with cheese curds and gravy."

"No. The Canadians invented fried dough, too."

"I thought fried dough came from Italy," said Maggie. "You know—zeppoles."

Luigi didn't say anything. He was too busy remembering something else Professor Marvelmous had told him.

"It's a treasure hunt!"

"Huh?" said his friends.

"When I was thinking about creating a treasure hunt, Professor Marvelmous told me the clues would be better if they rhymed."

"Well, this one sure does," said Chester.

"But it doesn't make much sense," said Maggie.

"We have to find the hidden meanings," Luigi explained.

Maggie handed him the card. "Go for it."

Luigi studied the words carefully. "'The land of fried dough . . .'"

"Canada," said Chester just as Maggie said, "Italy."

Luigi shook his head. "Nope. The fairgrounds."

"The funnel cakes!" said Chester.

"Yep," said Luigi.

"But what about this guy he must've met?" Maggie wondered. "Mr. Johnny Pump won't still be there. The carnival's closed."

"Maybe Johnny Pump means something else," said Luigi.

"Quick!" said Chester. "To the library. Mrs. Tobin will

know. She's a librarian. They know everything. And if they don't, they know how to learn it!"

They raced to the library. Mrs. Tobin looked pointedly at Luigi's hat.

"Oops, sorry!" He pulled it off.

"A johnny pump is an old-fashioned New York City name for a fire hydrant," Mrs. Tobin told them after consulting some reference books.

"Thanks, Mrs. Tobin!" they all said as they headed for the door.

"Aren't you three going to check out any books?"

"Not today," said Luigi.

"We're on a quest!" said Maggie.

"Aha," said Mrs. Tobin. "Quest on, my Frodos. Quest on!"

The three friends caught their breath in the shade of Fusilli's oak tree.

"Now we have to find a graveyard with a fire hydrant," said Chester.

Luigi and Maggie gawked at him.

"Because there's a guy named Professor Plum buried three feet in front of the fire hydrant's face," said Chester. "Remember?"

"Chester?" said Luigi.

"Yeah?"

"You need to play more board games. Professor Plum is a character from Clue!"

"Aha!" said Maggie. "So there's another 'clue' buried three feet in front of the face of a fire hydrant somewhere on the fairgrounds."

"Probably near where I bought my funnel cakes," said Chester.

"We need a shovel!" said Maggie.

"No," said Luigi. "A hand trowel. If someone asks why we're digging a hole, we can say we're planting flowers!"

"The super has gardening tools in his workshop," said Chester. "He'll let us borrow them."

When Chester said "gardening," Luigi remembered seeing Professor Marvelmous on the day of the sidewalk board-game fiasco.

The knees of his trousers had been caked with dirt.

The professor had explained that he'd done "a little gardening." That he'd been "planting seeds for a glorious future."

He probably meant Maggie's future!

This treasure, whatever it was, had to be super important. It might even change Maggie's whole life.

Luigi had to help her find it!

Moving quickly, the three friends raced back to the alley to grab the hand trowel and then hurried over to the fairgrounds.

In some places, they could still see tire treads stamped into the mud or flattened grass where the big rides had been erected.

"Where was the funnel-cake guy?" Luigi asked.

"I'm not exactly sure," said Chester. "It all looks so different."

"Concentrate," said Maggie. "Please?"

"Okay. I remember we could see the balloon booth."

"That was over there," said Luigi, who knew its position well.

"Near the picnic table," added Maggie.

"Right," said Chester. "Then we had to walk around a popcorn booth." He marked off the steps.

Luigi saw a clump of crushed white kernels smooshed into the dirt.

"Past the corn-dog stand," said Chester. "To . . . there!"

He pointed to a fire hydrant.

"The funnel-cake guy was right in front of what I now like to call a johnny pump."

They hurried over to it.

"We have to dig three feet in front of its face," said Maggie.

"Where's the face?" asked Chester.

The three friends walked around the hydrant.

"Here we go," said Luigi. "That big round thing on the front with the locknut is the nose. The smaller knobs on either side are the ears. And the dome up top is its head."

Maggie walked out three paces and marked an X into the dirt with the trowel.

She dropped to her knees and started digging.

She'd barely turned over four scoops of soil when

someone ding-a-linged a bike bell while someone else honked a bike horn.

Chad Chiltington and Jimmy Willoughby came charging across the open field on their wheelie bikes.

They both slammed on their coaster brakes and skidded to a grass-slashing stop.

"What are you three juvenile delinquents up to this time?" demanded Chiltington.

Willoughby sneered. "Or should we just call the cops so you can tell *them* why you're digging an illegal hole on public property?"

Not again, thought Luigi.

But instead of panicking or running away or cowering in fear, Luigi politely doffed his top hat.

"Why are you still wearing that stupid thing?" demanded Willoughby.

"Because, my good man, it suits me."

"I oughta flatten it!" said Chiltington. He slammed a fist into his open palm.

Bullies, thought Luigi. *They think they can push and shove and scare anyone into doing anything.*

It was time to push back.

"Oh, do you want to play rock-paper-scissors, Chad? Perhaps later. Right now, I think it's splenderrific that you two fine fellows bicycled all the way over here to offer us your kind assistance."

"Huh?" said Chiltington.

"I'm sure your parents will be pleased as punch—the kind made with ginger ale and sherbet—that you have volunteered to join us in our community beautification project."

"Your what?" said Willoughby.

"Community beautification project. A CBP, not to be confused with CBS, home to several fine television programs and, of course, the *CBS Evening News.*"

"What the heck are you jabbering about?" said Chiltington.

"How, working together, the five of us shall turn these fairgrounds into marvelously spectacular grounds by planting all manner of bulbs to bloom in the spring. We've only kept it hush-hush because . . ."

Luigi nodded toward the nearby trees.

"We didn't want the local squirrels to know what we're up to. Squirrels do love digging up plump and juicy tulip bulbs, do they not?"

He bounced on the balls of his feet, wishing he already had a pair of banana shoes to punctuate his remarks with a rude and gassy bleat.

"You three are planting flowers?" sneered Chiltington.

"Bulbs, Chadwick. Bulbs. Not the kind you screw into lamps, mind you, or the rubber bubble at the business end of a turkey baster. No, these bulbs are the kind that blossom into tulips, the same kind of flower that grows upon your face."

Chiltington and Willoughby were eyeballing Luigi.

"You're a dipstick," said Willoughby.

"A true weirdo," added Chiltington.

"I thank you for that compliment, good sirs," said Luigi, bending into a bow.

"I'm outta here," said Chad. "I need to go to work at my stupid new job."

"So what am I supposed to do all day?" whined Jimmy. "My old man has *me* working the night shift."

The two boys pedaled away.

"Wow," said Chester when Willoughby and Chiltington disappeared behind the trees. "The mouth is, indeed, mightier than the sword. You really took care of those two."

"This is *our* game," said Luigi. "This time, Chiltington and Willoughby don't get to write the rules."

When the coast was clear, Maggie went back to her digging.

"What in the world did Uncle Clarence bury here?" she said.

"I think it could be something huge," said Luigi.

"We should've taken the bigger shovel," said Chester.

"I mean, like a college scholarship or something."

"Or a plane ticket to Paris!" said Maggie. She dug faster, piling up a mound of clay, dirt, and rocks off to one side. About two feet down, the tip of the trowel struck something metal.

"A treasure chest!" exclaimed Chester.

"No," said Maggie, scraping away the soil. "It looks more like a rusty old Band-Aid box."

"Which is where Professor Marvelmous always used to store his money," said Luigi.

"Is it enough to pay for college?" wondered Chester. "How about a ticket to Paris?"

Maggie raised the hinged lid of the Band-Aid box . . .

. . . and pulled out a plastic sandwich baggie.

There was a yellow note card sealed inside.

"Aha," said Luigi. "Another clue. The game is afoot."

"How can a game also be a foot?" asked Chester.

"It's just something Sherlock Holmes says when he gets excited. What's the clue?"

Maggie read the card: "'Andrew Carnegie gave you this little piece of heaven. Fly there now and check out a seven-three-seven.'"

"Awesome!" said Chester. "We need to fly on the new Boeing seven-thirty-seven jet. Of course, we may need to go to Germany first. According to *Popular Mechanics,* Lufthansa is the only airline currently flying the new jet."

"Good to know," said Luigi. "But this clue is directing us back to the library. Remember? It was donated to the town by that legendary rich guy Andrew Carnegie."

"So what's the seven-thirty-seven?" asked Maggie.

"The first part of a Dewey decimal number?" suggested Chester.

Luigi nodded. "It's a possibility. Maggie? Can you stash

my top hat in your backpack? I'm not supposed to wear it inside the library. And we're gonna need more help from Mrs. Tobin to find our next clue."

"Don't worry," said Chester. "Like I said, she's a librarian. Helping people find stuff is what librarians do best!"

"Only two requests have ever been made for a book with a seven-three-seven code on its spine during all my years here at the library," said Mrs. Tobin. "One from you three and another from the gentleman who came in here last week."

"Did he have big bushy eyebrows, a curled mustache, chubby chipmunk cheeks, and a sly twinkle in his eyes?" asked Luigi.

"Yes."

"Was he also extremely charming?" asked Maggie.

"Oh, yes," said Mrs. Tobin, blushing slightly. "Very charming indeed. Follow me, please."

The librarian led Luigi, Maggie, and Chester to the shelves housing her small collection of books with Dewey decimal numbers starting with a seven. "Seven-three, of course, refers to sculpture. Seven-three-seven further refines the categorization to books about numismatics, coins, and medals—all of which include items that are engraved, a form of sculpture."

"Because Uncle Clarence is a coin collector!" said Maggie.

Mrs. Tobin peered over the frames of her glasses. "Uncle Clarence?"

"He performed as Professor Marvelmous at the summer carnival," explained Luigi.

"Ah, yes. Your merry and jocular employer. Is that who visited me to request this tome?"

"We think so," said Luigi.

"Fascinating."

She reached for a bright red leather-bound book with 737.324 stamped on its spine.

"Here we are." She handed the book to Maggie.

Maggie read the title embossed in gold type on the cover. "*A Guide Book of United States Coins,* Twentieth Edition, 1967."

"Coin collectors often refer to this as the Official Red Book. It lists collectible coins and their current value," said Mrs. Tobin. "Oh my."

"What?" said Luigi.

"It seems the last patron to browse through this book, presumably Maggie's uncle, used a greeting card to mark their place."

She pulled the bright purple envelope out of the book.

"The envelope is addressed to you, Maggie. Oh, I wish people wouldn't use glitter powder when slipping secret messages into books."

Mrs. Tobin blew a few sparkle flakes off the page and handed the envelope to Maggie.

"Wait a second," said Luigi. "What's on the page Professor Marvelmous bookmarked?"

"Good question," said Chester. "It could be a clue too."

Mrs. Tobin arched an eyebrow. "A clue for what?"

"We're on a treasure hunt," said Chester.

"Maggie's uncle organized the whole thing for her," said Luigi.

"I have a bunch of uncles," said Maggie. "But he's the fun and wacky one."

"Ah, yes," said Mrs. Tobin. "We all need one of those."

"So, what's on the page?" asked Luigi.

Mrs. Tobin laid the book down on a table. It was open to a page with an article about rare pennies.

"Fascinating," she said, running her finger underneath the text. "In 1943, pennies were supposed to be made from stainless steel instead of copper because copper was needed for military purposes during World War Two. However, a few very rare pennies were struck by accident when some copper-alloy one-cent blanks remained in the press hopper as production began on the new steel pennies. There are only about forty still in existence. Oh my."

"What?" said Maggie eagerly.

"A 1943 copper one-cent coin was offered for sale ten years ago, in 1958. It sold for more than forty thousand dollars!"

Everyone's jaw dropped when Mrs. Tobin said that. You could definitely go to college *and* fly to Paris with forty thousand dollars. You could probably go both places twice.

"How much might it be worth today?" asked Chester.

Mrs. Tobin laughed. "More."

The three friends sat down with the red book as Mrs. Tobin went off to help another patron.

"Maggie?" Luigi whispered. "I think a 1943 copper penny is the treasure your uncle Clarence wants you to find. Remember the first rhyme? 'Pardon my pun . . .'"

Maggie gasped. "'But this is the big *one*!' A penny that's worth a whole lot more than one cent."

"I think it might be at the bank," said Luigi.

"How come?" said Maggie.

"You weren't at the carnival yet. But my family solved one of the Balloon-centration puzzles. The answer was 'laugh all the way to the bank.' Your uncle said, 'I already did so today.'"

"You're kidding," said Maggie. "He took an extremely rare penny to the bank and deposited it for me? I don't even have a bank account."

"Maybe *he* does," said Luigi.

"Wait," said Chester. "If Professor Marvelmous deposited

the special coin into his account, the actual penny would disappear into a pile with all the bank's other pennies. Your uncle would simply have one cent added to his balance."

"Let's not get ahead of ourselves," suggested Luigi. "Let's just play the game, one turn at a time. Maggie? Open the envelope. We need the next clue!"

"We have another rebus," said Maggie, pulling a yellow card out of the purple envelope.

Mrs. Tobin passed by and peeked at the card over Maggie's shoulder.

"Oh my. It looks like one of those puzzles from that TV game show."

"*Concentration,*" said Chester. "We used to watch it at Bruno's place all the time."

"Where is Bruno?" asked Mrs. Tobin.

"Long story," said Luigi.

"Sad one, too," added Chester.

"Let's save it for another time," said Luigi. "We need to press on. Thanks for all your help, Mrs. Tobin."

"You're welcome. Good luck on your quest!"

Luigi headed out the front door. Chester and Maggie followed him.

"So, uh, where are we going?" asked Chester.

"We need to be back at the fairgrounds," said Luigi.

"You already solved that rebus puzzle?" asked Maggie.

"It's what he does best," remarked Chester.

"What does it say?" asked Maggie.

"It says, 'Dig—'"

He didn't say anything else.

Because Jimmy Willoughby was in the street, swooping back and forth, doing a figure eight on his bike.

"I know you three twerps are up to something!" he shouted. "And I'm going to find out what it is! I'm going to follow you all day long!"

"I can't stand that guy," whispered Maggie.

"That makes it unanimous," said Chester.

"This is like chess or checkers," said Luigi. "We need to think several moves ahead of our opponent."

"Well, we know he's going to keep tailing us on that bike," said Maggie. "So when I find Uncle Clarence's treasure . . ."

"He'll come up with some reason to snatch it away," said Luigi. "And his night janitor job doesn't start till seven. That's when my dad had to be at the department store."

They walked up the sidewalk. Jimmy Willoughby shadowed them on his bike.

"In other words," said Chester, "he can keep bugging us all day long."

They were all keeping their voices low so Willoughby couldn't hear them.

"This is our game," said Luigi. "And I have an idea about how to deal Jimmy a clunker card and take him off the board for a turn or two. Maggie, can you get your hands on a curly black wig?"

"How curly?"

Luigi fluffed up his own hair. "This curly."

"No problem."

"Chester? Is the Pump 'N' Pedal bike as awesome as you and Dad were hoping?"

"Oh yeah. That thing's fast. Twice as fast as any normal bike."

Luigi did a slight head bob to indicate Willoughby. "Including his?"

"Totally. Those banana seat bikes are made for popping wheelies, not for high-speed chases."

"Excellent."

"But wait a second," said Chester. "What does that last clue tell us to do?"

Maggie pulled the rebus puzzle out of her backpack and held it in front of Luigi and Chester, making sure to shield it from anybody sneaking up behind them, like Jimmy Willoughby:

Usually, Luigi would let the others guess an answer first. But the clock was ticking.

"'Dig three feet west from the first hole,'" he said. "It's sending us back to the fairgrounds. Chester?"

"Yeah?"

"I need to borrow the Pump 'N' Pedal."

"Sure. I parked it in the alley."

"Cool. Maggie? I also need my top hat."

She pulled it out of her backpack. Luigi put it on.

"How long will it take you to get that wig?" he asked her.

"Five, ten minutes tops."

"Okay. Chester? You go with Maggie. Willoughby can't follow all of us, so I'm pretty sure he'll stick with me. I'll meet you two at the fairgrounds in fifteen minutes. And, Chester?"

"Yeah?"

"Put on the curly-haired wig."

"How come?"

"We're gonna need you to be me."

"Hey, come back here, Lemon Head!" shouted Willoughby.

Luigi tore out of the alley and up the street on the incredible Pump 'N' Pedal bicycle. Willoughby had been lurking down the block, waiting for Luigi to make his next move in their game of cat and mouse.

Now he was desperately trying to keep up with the amazingly turbocharged ride that Chester and Luigi's dad had engineered and built. With the extra boost of power from the pumpable handlebars—which Luigi worked like oars on a rowboat—the new bike left Willoughby's wheelie popper in its dust.

Luigi navigated the bike toward the fairgrounds.

When he got there, Chester and Maggie were standing by. Chester had on the wig.

Luigi brought the two-wheeled speedster to a tire-smoking stop.

"Wow! This thing is fast!" he shouted.

He hopped off and handed Chester his jean jacket and top hat.

"Okay, you're me," he said.

"Impossible," said Chester. "You're one of a kind, Luigi."

Luigi laughed. "You too, Chester. And this bike? Awesometastic. Okay. Get ready. Willoughby should be coming up the road any second. Just don't let him get in front of you and see your face."

"Ha," said Chester, climbing aboard the Pump 'N' Pedal. "Not gonna happen!"

Chester rode out into the street.

Maggie and Luigi hid behind a shrub.

They waited. And waited.

Finally Willoughby arrived, huffing and puffing.

"Get . . . back . . . here . . . Lemon . . ."

Chester blasted off, working the pumping handlebars hard. Willoughby chased after him.

"Come on!" said Luigi when the two bikes were gone. "There's where we dug the first hole."

Luigi led the way to the semi-bald spot in the sea of grass surrounding the fire hydrant.

"I'll mark off three paces," said Maggie. She did. Then she dropped to her knees and started digging.

About a foot down, the blade of her trowel tapped another Band-Aid box.

"I found it!" she announced.

Luigi helped her clean away the dirt.

Maggie wedged the metal box out of its snug hiding spot with the tip of the gardening tool. She popped open the lid.

"Another sandwich bag," she reported. "This one has a key inside it!"

She pulled out the small and oddly shaped key. It had a round head and a long rectangular blade with square ridges and teeth.

"'The Gold Leaf Bank' is etched into it."

"What's on that tag?" asked Luigi.

"The number one-seven-six." She showed Luigi the plastic oval, which was attached to the key with a paper-clip-thin key ring.

"Of course," said Luigi. "Professor Marvelmous didn't put the rare penny into his bank account. He kept it secure in one of the bank's safe-deposit boxes."

"Remember that thing Uncle Clarence said?" asked Maggie.

"He said so many memorable things. . . ."

"He told me that spending time with you guys had been 'stupendously good' for me. That it might even prove to be the *key* to my future! Well, Luigi, we just dug up that key!"

Maggie slipped the key into the pocket of her jeans. Luigi helped her refill the hole. Then they both took off, jogging back to Poplar Lane, where they'd rendezvous with Chester.

He arrived in the alley about five minutes after they did.

"I lost Willoughby like an hour ago," Chester boasted as he climbed off the bike. He peeled off the jean jacket and handed it and the top hat to Luigi. He plucked the curly wig off his head and gave it to Maggie—after using it like a mop to swipe away some sweat.

"I let him chase me all through town," Chester continued. "Lots of folks were admiring my ride. A couple times, I had to wait by the curb so Willoughby could catch up with me. This one guy in a business suit offered to buy the bike. I told him, 'Get in line. It's a one-of-a-kind, custom-made Raymo-Lemoncello!'"

"I really think this is going to work!" Luigi told Maggie and Chester the next morning.

Fusilli barked in agreement.

The dog would be tagging along for the game's final roll of the dice. Maggie was just a few spaces away from victory!

They'd gathered in the alley behind the apartment building. The plan was to walk downtown to the bank. Chester had already scouted out the street on his speedy bike. Jimmy Willoughby was nowhere to be seen. One exhausting chase scene with the Pump 'N' Pedal was probably more than he ever wanted. Luigi imagined that the poor guy's leg muscles were really screaming at him this morning.

Once they reached the Gold Leaf Bank, Maggie would march in with her key, go to the safe-deposit box, and retrieve the puzzle box's grand prize: the 1943 copper penny that was worth more than forty thousand dollars.

"I can't thank you guys enough," said Maggie as they strolled toward downtown.

"Hey, it's been fun," said Chester.

"And if we've had fun," added Luigi, "then we've already won."

As he said it, Luigi realized something. He didn't have to score the victory or take home the big prize. It wasn't even about making money. He loved making games even more than playing or winning them. For Luigi, the real joy came from giving joy to other people.

As they walked, Luigi's pockets jingled and jangled.

"What's all that clinking?" asked Chester.

"My pockets are full of nickels, dimes, and quarters," Luigi explained. "Professor Marvelmous paid me with a ton of coins. Once Maggie picks up her penny, I thought I might ask a teller to roll them up and exchange the coins for paper money."

Five minutes later the friends were standing in front of the very impressive Gold Leaf Bank.

It was a three-story-tall granite fortress that took up half a downtown block. At its peak sat a shimmering gold dome. There were no windows in the boxy building. Just an arched and heavy front door off a landing reached by a short flight of three marble steps.

"You ever wonder why the bank doesn't have any windows?" asked Chester.

Luigi shrugged. "Probably to keep bank robbers from busting in."

"I can't do it!" Maggie suddenly blurted.

"What?" said Luigi and Chester.

"Come with me, Luigi. You can do all the talking. You're good at talking."

Luigi remembered how Maggie had reacted the first time they'd won the radio-station treasure hunt. She hadn't wanted to go on the air.

"I told you—I'm more of a behind-the-scenes person," she said. "What if there's a bank guard? What if somebody tries to stop me? What if I don't know what to say? You *always* know what to say."

"Okay, okay," Luigi told her. "Chester? You stay out here and take care of Fusilli."

Chester nodded. "Got it."

Luigi and Maggie both took a deep breath and sprinted up the marble steps to the bank entrance. Luigi heaved open the heavy front door. It creaked on its hinges. When they stepped into the grand foyer, Luigi felt like he had just entered the Temple of Money.

There was a humongous oil portrait of a scowling old man hanging on a wall over a double-door entrance into the bank's main floor.

"Who's that?" whispered Maggie.

Luigi squinted so he could read the plaque bolted to the bottom edge of the gilded frame.

"'Our beloved bank president,'" he said. "'Mr. Chauncy Q. Chiltington.'"

"Chad's father," said Maggie.

Luigi nodded.

Mr. Chiltington looked super serious. Super sour. His eyes were beady and hard, as if he suspected that everyone who dared enter this building was some sort of bum or thief.

Luigi and Maggie pulled open the double doors and stepped into a wide-open rotunda topped by a dome. The bank was creepily quiet. The whole stony place shimmered and gleamed. But not the people. They were all frowning like Mr. Chiltington's portrait. Maybe it was bank policy.

Brass poles and red velvet ropes marked off lanes for sad-faced customers to shuffle up to the barred teller cages. Two burly security guards in navy-blue blazers gave Luigi and Maggie a look.

Maybe kids aren't allowed in the bank?

Maggie whistled to calm her nerves. Luigi looked around for a sign that might point them to the safe-deposit boxes.

There.

Over by the curving staircase leading down into the basement.

"This way," he whispered to Maggie.

She handed him the key. "Take it," she told him. "My hands are too sweaty. The key could slip."

"Don't worry," said Luigi, taking the key. "There's nothing to be nervous about. We don't need to talk to a teller. We'll just go downstairs, find box one-seventy-six, open it, and—"

"What are you two doing here?"

It was Chad Chiltington. Dressed in dark green coveralls and pushing a broom.

So *this* was the job Chiltington's father had found for him.

"I—uh—we have a key," Maggie stammered.

Luigi held it up. "It's for a safe-deposit box."

"No it's not. Guards? Security?"

The two burly men in blue blazers came over to see what the problem was.

"These two are known troublemakers," Chad told them. "My father would not like seeing them inside his bank."

"Yes, sir, Mr. Chiltington," said the one guard.

"We'll take care of it, sir," said the other.

"Let's go," the first guard said to Luigi.

"Nice and easy," the other one said to Maggie.

"But I have a key," Maggie protested.

"Yeah? Me too. It's for my car. Got another one for my house."

The guards grabbed Maggie and Luigi under their arms

and unceremoniously hoisted them off the ground. They were hauled through the double doors, across the fancy foyer, and out of the bank.

"Children aren't allowed downstairs with the safe-deposit boxes," said the second guard. "Come back when you turn eighteen!"

"Sorry," Luigi said to Maggie as Chester and Fusilli rushed over to join them.

"Are you guys okay?" asked Chester.

"Yeah," said Luigi.

"Enough is enough," said a furious Maggie.

Luigi wondered if her rage was what Bruno had felt before his big betrayal. Maybe he'd decided that if he couldn't beat the Chiltingtons and Willoughbys, he might as well join them.

But Luigi knew the game was never over until it was over!

"My treasure is in that bank," fumed Maggie. "And I'm not going to let anybody stop me from getting it, not even Chad Chiltington."

"Chad Chiltington's in there?" said Chester.

Luigi nodded. "This is the job his father found him. Pushing a broom at the bank."

"He sicced the security guards on us," added Maggie.

"We're gonna need a new game plan," said Luigi. "Kids aren't allowed downstairs, and that's where the safe-deposit boxes are."

For a second, he could've sworn that Professor Marvelmous was standing right there in front of him, swirling his hand to make a grand pronouncement: *Don't hide your light under a bushel, my boy, especially one filled with apples. Use your gift, Luigi. Use it well!*

"Luigi?" said Maggie, sounding worried.

"Hmmm?"

"You look kind of dazed," said Chester.

"No. I'm fine. What happened in there was a minor setback. A 'go back three spaces' card. A detour to the molasses swamp in Candy Land."

Maggie arched an eyebrow. "You still play Candy Land?"

"Yes. But only with my little sister Sofia. We need to create a distraction." He looked down at Fusilli, who was panting eagerly and wagging his tail. "And this time, we're all going in."

"We are?" said Chester.

"Yep. Even Fusilli."

Maggie grinned. "What's the plan?"

"I need my top hat."

Maggie dug it out of her backpack.

"Follow my lead. We're going to create a scene."

"Um, what exactly is the objective of this scene we're going to create?" asked Chester.

"To keep the guards busy," said Luigi. "Chad Chiltington, too. Since the safe-deposit boxes are downstairs . . ."

Maggie finished Luigi's thought. "We keep everybody occupied *upstairs* while one of us sneaks *downstairs* to pick up my penny."

"Exactly." Luigi brandished his invisible sword. "Fun for all!"

"And all for fun!" shouted Chester and Maggie. Fusilli just barked.

Luigi led the charge up the three marble steps.

He pulled open the heavy front door.

They stepped into the foyer.

Luigi looked down at his dog. "You ready, boy?"

Fusilli sat down on the cold stone floor and smiled from ear to fuzzy ear.

"Good! Because it's showtime!"

"No weirdos allowed!" shouted Chad. "No dogs, either!"

Luigi, Chester, Maggie, and Fusilli stepped into the bank's rotunda.

"I thought we told you two to leave!" said the burliest of the two hulking security guards.

"Indeed you did, good sir," said Luigi, bowing and doffing his top hat. "However, I forgot: I need to open a bank account for my dog."

"What?" said the guard.

"He's quite famous. I'm sure you've seen his face on dog-food cans. Dog-food bags. Flea-and-tick-collar displays, perhaps?"

"Get out of my father's bank!" shouted Chad.

Luigi put a hand to his heart as his face filled with concern.

"Heavens, Chadwick. Do you mean to say your father

and the Gold Leaf Bank won't open a savings account for anyone who wants to open one?"

Some of the bank's customers, waiting in those roped-off lines, turned to see what all the fuss was about.

"Isn't that a violation of several federal banking regulations?" said Chester, using his loud, shouting-up-four-stories voice.

"I think it is illegal!" bellowed Maggie. Her voice was even louder.

"I said get out of here!" screamed Chiltington. "All of you!"

"But I just want to open a bank account for my very famous dog!" said Luigi.

"Your dog isn't famous!" snapped Chiltington.

Fusilli growled.

"Oh dear," said Luigi. "Now you've gone and insulted him."

A man in a pin-striped suit bustled over to see what was causing the commotion in the tomb-quiet rotunda.

"Young man," he said. "I'm Harold Billingsly, bank manager. Kindly lower your voice."

"Why?" shouted Luigi. "I've found that people can hear me much better when I raise it. *YOU* HEARD ME, RIGHT?"

"He wants to open a bank account for his dog," said Maggie matter-of-factly.

"And his dog is famous," said Chester.

"Wh-wh-what?" sputtered the manager. "No bank in

America would open a savings account for a dog, no matter how famous he or she might be."

"Oh, I see," said Luigi with a polite smile. "You thought I wanted to open the account in *his* name. No, sir. Of course not. After all . . ."

Luigi shaded his mouth with his hand so as not to offend Fusilli.

"He *is* a dog. But I, as his agent, manager, and primary poop scooper, would like to open one of your famous Young Savers Accounts." Luigi gestured to a framed poster advertising the special promotion. "That way I can hold his earnings in trust, which is much better than holding them in rust, which can really leave a stain on your hands. I'd also like the free transistor radio that comes with every new account. I brought along our first deposit."

Luigi reached deep into both of his pockets and yanked them open. All the jingling coins he'd been carrying flew out and skittered across the floor.

Chester and Maggie dropped to their knees. Luigi flicked his shoe to "accidentally" sideswipe a pile to the right and then to the left, expanding the sea of coins.

"This floor is so slick!" said Chester, shoving another cluster of coins across the floor.

"The coins keep sliding away from me," said Maggie, giving the ones closest to her a good nudge.

"Mr. Chiltington?" snapped the bank manager. "Kindly sweep up this coinage immediately."

Chad came over with his push broom.

Which looked pretty threatening to Fusilli.

So he snarled and lunged forward.

Chad retreated a step.

"I hate dogs!" he shouted. "Guards!"

They came charging over.

And slipped on all the loose change scattered across the buffed, glassy floor.

They landed on their butts.

Customers hurried over to help the guards and the kids. Some of them skated across the coins and tumbled.

"You still have the key?" Maggie whispered to Luigi.

He nodded.

"Go for it!"

So, while everyone was distracted, Luigi raced over to the steps and headed down to the basement.

Behind him, he heard Fusilli barking, coins clinking, Chiltington blubbering, and Mr. Billingsly shouting at the two bank guards to "do something."

When Luigi reached the basement, he saw a gigantic bank-vault door. A ten-foot-tall circle of steel, it had a large, spindled wheel at its center.

Cool, he thought.

But Luigi wasn't there for the bank vault. A sign indicated that the safe-deposit room was down the hall to the left. Luigi ran. He didn't know how much longer Fusilli, Chester, and Maggie could keep everybody occupied upstairs.

He darted into the empty room. There was an entire

wall of what looked like stacked apartment-building mail-boxes. Each one was numbered. Fortunately, 176 wasn't too high off the floor. Luigi could reach it.

He pulled out his key, slid it into a key slot . . .

And realized something that made his heart sink.

You needed *two* keys to unlock the box!

"Are you in need of assistance, young man?" asked a sweet voice behind Luigi.

A bank employee with short black hair had entered the safe-deposit room and closed its door behind her. She looked vaguely familiar. She was also holding a very familiar-looking key.

"As you may not know," the lady said with a smile, "safe-deposit boxes are protected by two keys. One that the bank gives to the renter of the box. And another 'guard key' that the bank keeps. Without both, the box cannot be opened."

"This is Professor Marvelmous's box," Luigi explained.

"Of course. The wonderfully entertaining gentleman who ran the balloon-pop booth at the summer carnival. And you are Luigi, his assistant."

"Yes, ma'am." He was a little surprised that the lady recognized him. "The contents of this box are supposed to go to his niece, Maggie . . . I mean Margaret Keeley."

"And you're helping her retrieve them?"

"Yes, ma'am."

"Just like you helped my son."

"Excuse me?"

"You were wonderful with him when he finally mustered up the courage to play that balloon game in front of the carnival crowd. Remember? You had him write down his answer instead of saying it out loud, because, in my opinion, you're a very nice young man. Vinny's told me all about how you look after him at the library."

Everything finally clicked. "You're Vinny's mom! Mrs. Ciccarelli! You were at the booth with him."

"Yes. I manage the safe-deposit box room for the Gold Leaf Bank. Children really aren't allowed in here. But since you bent the rules for Vinny, I think I can bend them a little for you." She marched crisply to the wall of metal boxes and slipped her key into the second slot on box 176. "Thank you, Luigi," she said with a smile. "From the bottom of my heart."

She twisted her key. Luigi twisted his. The rectangular door swung open. Mrs. Ciccarelli extracted a long metal tray. As she pulled it out, Luigi could hear what sounded like a single penny sliding around inside it.

"When you're done, simply leave the tray on the counter."

Mrs. Ciccarelli smiled and exited the room.

Luigi raised the lid on the long tray. The first thing he saw was another purple note card.

Dearest Maggie,

I have no children of my own. But I've always wanted to send one to college. Maybe Paris. How about New York, Milan, and London, too? I want to help you live your dream, Maggie. Because I believe in YOU. Always have. Always will. Your future will be wondermous. Because you already are.

Love,
Uncle Clarence

Luigi couldn't believe what an incredible gift the professor was giving his only niece. A college scholarship? A chance for her to study in the fashion capitals of the world? Maybe, someday Luigi could give a gift like this to someone else. Maybe even a whole bunch of college scholarships!

He plucked the card out of the tray, and there it was. One very rare 1943 copper penny.

Sure, there were billions of pennies in the world, but

every now and then, one came along that was different. Peculiar. Maybe even odd.

And that was what made it so special.

Luigi might've been imagining things, but this particular penny seemed to glow.

Carefully, very carefully, he tucked it into his jeans. He used that special pocket-watch pocket, because he figured that was what Maggie would do. He slid Professor Marvelmous's card into a second pocket. He placed the empty tray on the counter, left the room, and zipped back up the stairs with a penny worth over forty thousand dollars. When he reached the main floor, nobody was there.

Well, the customers and bank tellers were, but he didn't see Chester, Maggie, or Fusilli.

He didn't see Chad Chiltington, Mr. Billingsly, or the two brawny bank guards, either.

Luigi raced through the double doors, across the foyer, and out the entrance.

"Here he comes!" said Maggie, pointing at Luigi.

She, Chester, and Fusilli were standing next to the WALX Prize Patrol van. Chester held a bulging paper sack. Someone must've lent him their lunch bag to hold all of Luigi's coins.

Chad Chiltington, the two bank guards, and Mr. Billingsly were standing off to the side, glowering at them.

A man wearing headphones and holding a WALX microphone saw Luigi coming down the steps and said, "This is Brian Britain, WALX News. We're here, live, with Luigi

Lemoncello. The thirteen-year-old boy who, we're told, just proved that a penny saved is a penny earned."

"I'm just the coin courier," said Luigi. "This is Maggie Keeley's penny. A gift from her uncle Clarence."

Luigi handed Maggie the penny and the note card.

"Thank you, Luigi!" She glanced at the card. "Oh my," she gasped. Her uncle's message seemed to be choking her up.

But she quickly composed herself and triumphantly brandished the shiny copper penny and held it high.

The radio newsman turned his attention to her. "And you are?"

"Maggie Keeley."

"Maggie, can you tell our WALX listeners about this penny? What makes it so special?"

"It's unique. You see, back in 1943 . . ."

While Maggie talked about the penny and its history, Luigi drifted over to where Chester was petting Fusilli.

"You need to give Fusilli some special treats tonight," said Chester. "He kept them all running around in circles. It was hilarious."

Luigi nodded toward the radio newscaster interviewing Maggie. "This is brilliant. Chiltington and the bank manager can't make a scene or give us any grief. Not in front of the news guy."

"Exactly," said Chester.

"So how did Brian Britain know to be here? How'd they know I had the penny?"

Chester grinned. "I had a few coins in my pocket too. So when you and Maggie went into the bank that first time, I found a pay phone and made a call to WALX. You're not the only one who's always thinking two moves ahead, Luigi."

Maggie Keeley promised Luigi and his whole family that she would loan them whatever they needed just as soon as she found a numismatist to sell her rare penny.

"She means a coin dealer," Luigi explained.

There was a big celebration early that evening out in the alley. Everyone was so proud of Luigi, Chester, and Maggie. They'd done the impossible: they'd gone up against the Chiltingtons and Willoughbys and won. They'd even been on the news!

Mrs. Lemoncello made her famous lemon-berry fizz. The neighbors rolled out charcoal grills and sizzled hot dogs and hamburgers for everybody. Luigi's brothers and sisters took turns riding the Pump 'N' Pedal bicycle around the block.

And there were balloons. Lots of them. Tied off in bunches to all the fire escapes.

Luigi and Chester were standing next to a grill when a surprise guest arrived.

"Um, hey, guys."

It was Bruno.

"Hey," said Chester, somewhat hesitantly.

"Bruno!" Luigi exclaimed as he threw open his arms.

Because he remembered something else Professor Marvelmous had told him: *We must have compassion for those who have not yet journeyed as far as we have along this twisty, turny path we call life.*

"Fun for all?" Luigi said to his longtime friend, who, yes, had made a very serious mistake. But the professor had also said he'd learned so much from his mistakes that he wanted to make a few more.

Bruno nodded. "And all for fun!"

They embraced in a bear hug. Until Chester joined them. Then it was a group hug.

A few minutes later, Fabio came back to the alley on the Pump 'N' Pedal. He was trailed by a businessman in a finely tailored suit.

"Hey, that's the guy who wanted to buy the bike," Chester told Luigi. "When I was giving Jimmy Willoughby the runaround."

"I heard about that," said Bruno. "Wish I could've been there."

"Me too," said Chester.

"Excuse me," said the man in the business suit. "Is Mr. Lemoncello here?"

266

"Yes," said Luigi's father, wiping his hands on his apron. "I'm Angelo Lemoncello."

"I'm Charles Belkin," said the man, extending his hand. "I own the Belkin Bicycle Factory."

"I know," said Mr. Lemoncello with a grin. "I used to work for you."

"Really?"

Mr. Lemoncello shrugged. "The foreman let me go. Cutbacks. He said nobody wants to buy Belkin bikes anymore."

Mr. Belkin winced a little but nodded. "I'm afraid that is true. We're too old-fashioned. Nothing new or flashy. That's why I want to buy your idea. This Pump 'N' Pedal bike. I saw that young man over there riding it yesterday. It's an amazing feat of engineering."

Now Mr. Belkin had the whole neighborhood's attention.

"I'd like to mass-produce the Pump 'N' Pedal. Maybe call it the Belkin Blaster. We'd manufacture it right here in Alexandriaville. So I'd have to hire back a lot of my laid-off workers. Including you, Mr. Lemoncello."

"I'd have my old job back?" said Mr. Lemoncello.

Mr. Belkin shook his head. "No."

Luigi's shoulders slumped.

"You'd have a bigger, better job!" said Mr. Belkin. "With a bigger, better salary."

Fabio took that as his cue to jump in. "It'd have to be at least three times his old salary. Plus, Dad and Chester

267

Raymo, the bike's design engineer, would need to earn a royalty on every Belkin Blaster sold. Say, two percent, Mr. Belkin?"

Mr. Lemoncello beamed. "My son Fabio? He's sixteen. He's going to be a lawyer."

"Do you have a patent on this bike?" asked Mr. Belkin.

"Yes, sir," said Fabio. "We certainly do. I sent in all the forms. Paid all the fees."

"I see. You have a very impressive son," said Mr. Belkin.

"No," said Luigi's father, shaking his head. "I have *five* very impressive sons. And my five daughters? They're amazing too."

Mr. Belkin extended his hand. "So do we have a deal? Triple your old salary plus a two-percent royalty on every Belkin Blaster sold?"

Mr. Lemoncello looked at Chester. "You okay with that, Chester?"

Chester smiled. "Two percent works for me."

"Okay, Mr. Belkin," said Luigi's father. "We have a deal."

They shook hands on it. And Mr. Belkin stuck around long enough to enjoy a hot dog *and* a hamburger.

Epilogue

Every Saturday, Luigi would go to the Alexandriaville Public Library on Market Street by himself to work on board-game ideas.

He still went there during the week with Bruno, Chester, and Maggie to check out books and enjoy the air-conditioning. And he still found time to play his book scavenger-hunt game with Vinny.

But sleepy Saturdays were all about daydreaming and thinking up board-game ideas. And the library was the best place to do it.

"So, Luigi," asked Mrs. Tobin, "what's next?"

"I don't know. But I'd really like to finish designing this board game. I call it Family Frenzy. You're a member of a big family, where everybody is trying to find a way to stand out. To be Mom and Dad's favorite. You have to do things like sing a song. Dance. Tell a joke. Maybe solve a puzzle. But if you pull a clunker card, you lose a turn washing dishes or changing your baby sister's diapers. In the end, I want the players to figure out that they're better off working together instead of competing against each other. Because every player starts with a talent card that's different from everybody else's. You put them together? You're unstoppable."

"Sounds marvelous," said Mrs. Tobin. "You can work on Family Frenzy here at the library anytime it's open. And, as you know, my husband runs a printing press. If your game is half as good as I suspect it will be, perhaps he could run off a few copies."

"Thanks, Mrs. Tobin."

"Are those your playing pieces?" She gestured to a shoebox filled with plastic figurines.

"It's a start. I could use some more."

"How about a boot? For the dancer or fashion designer in the family. I have one in my desk drawer that someone left here years ago. I believe it's from a go-go Barbie doll."

She strolled back to her desk.

Luigi focused on the game board he was mapping out.

In fact he was so focused, so lost in his thoughts, that he didn't even look up when a police car with its siren wailing screamed past the library windows on its way to the Gold Leaf Bank, where bandits had just set off the burglar alarm.

But that's a story for another day.

A HIDDEN PUZZLE?

Like all Lemoncello stories, this one has a hidden puzzle. Here's a hint: Remember Luigi's first and worst idea for a game. When you find the solution, you're going to need this:

author@ChrisGrabenstein.com

Happy puzzling!

HEARTY AND SPLENDIFEROUS THANK-YOUS!

As always, there are so many people to thank for helping me with a new Lemoncello story.

A tip of the magical top hat to . . .

My wife, first reader, and *Shine!* coauthor, J.J. Thanks for letting me know my first outline for this prequel was a stinker. She was right. She usually is.

To my friends at Random House, especially Barbara Marcus, Michelle Nagler, and Shana Corey, who all said, "Hey, why don't we do a Lemoncello prequel?" I hadn't thought of that, but I'm glad *they* did!

Speaking of my editor, Shana, I cannot say enough about how much fun it is to work with her on these books. She gives the best notes and knows how to solve editorial puzzles with pinpoint, balloon-popping accuracy.

Shana also has a keen eye for talent and all-star editors of the future. Polo Orozco stepped up to assistant editor on this project, and I'm grateful for the extra pair of perceptive eyeballs.

Big thanks to my new agents, Carrie Hannigan and Josh Getzler, and their whole team at HG Literary. We're cooking up all sorts of exciting new things.

The cover artist, James Lancett, does such a great job capturing the spirit of a book in one simple graphic. I love all his work on the Lemoncello series, but this cover has a special place in my heart.

Thanks to the designers Michelle Cunningham (for the cover) and Larsson McSwain (for the interior).

Copyeditors Barbara Bakowski, Alison Kolani, and Jenica Nasworthy did their usual awesometastic job and made sure that Luigi's past jibed with his future.

Another tip of the top hat to managing editor Janet Foley, as well as production managers Tim Terhune and Shameiza Aly.

Oh, did I mention that this whole book, from start to finish, was done while everybody was working remotely during the COVID-19 lockdown? Thank you, Zoom. And Cisco Webex. And FaceTime. And . . . oh, you know who you are.

I'd also like to thank everybody in marketing, publicity, and sales who somehow found ways to keep getting books into kids' hands, even during the darkest days of bookstore closings, library shutdowns, and remote learning. Special thanks to John Adamo, Kathleen Dunn, Lili Feinberg, Kate Keating, Kelly McGauley, Shaughnessy

Miller, Janine Perez, Kristin Schulz, Erica Stone, and Adrienne Waintraub.

Finally, thank you to all the readers who have been with Mr. Lemoncello since the start. I hope you enjoyed this whole new beginning to his story!

NOW THAT YOU KNOW THIRTEEN-YEAR-OLD LUIGI L. LEMONCELLO . . .

SKIP AHEAD and read all about his splendiferous, **PUZZLE**-tastic games in the Mr. Lemoncello's Library books!

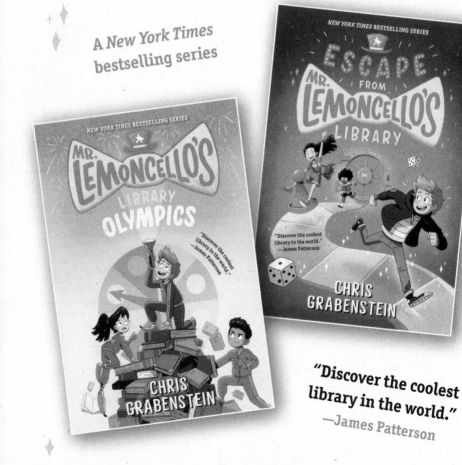

A *New York Times* bestselling series

★ "A worthy successor to the original madman puzzle-master himself, Willy Wonka."
—*Booklist*, starred review

IS IT FUN?
HELLO!
IT'S A
LEMONCELLO!

Turn the page for a sneak peek at Book 1.

This is how Kyle Keeley got grounded for a week.

First he took a shortcut through his mother's favorite rosebush.

Yes, the thorns hurt, but having crashed through the brambles and trampled a few petunias, he had a five-second jump on his oldest brother, Mike.

Both Kyle and his big brother knew exactly where to find what they needed to win the game: inside the house!

Kyle had already found the pinecone to complete his "outdoors" round. And he was pretty sure Mike had snagged his "yellow flower." Hey, it was June. Dandelions were everywhere.

"Give it up, Kyle!" shouted Mike as the brothers dashed up the driveway. "You don't stand a chance."

Mike zoomed past Kyle and headed for the front door, wiping out Kyle's temporary lead.

Of course he did.

Seventeen-year-old Mike Keeley was a total jock, a high school superstar. Football, basketball, baseball. If it had a ball, Mike Keeley was good at it.

Kyle, who was twelve, wasn't the star of anything.

Kyle's other brother, Curtis, who was fifteen, was still trapped over in the neighbor's yard, dealing with their dog. Curtis was the smartest Keeley. But for *his* "outdoors" round, he had pulled the always unfortunate Your Neighbor's Dog's Toy card. Any "dog" card was basically the same as a Lose a Turn.

As for why the three Keeley brothers were running around their neighborhood on a Sunday afternoon like crazed lunatics, grabbing all sorts of wacky stuff, well, it was their mother's fault.

She was the one who had suggested, "If you boys are bored, play a board game!"

So Kyle had gone down into the basement and dug up one of his all-time favorites: Mr. Lemoncello's Indoor-Outdoor Scavenger Hunt. It had been a huge hit for Mr. Lemoncello, the master game maker. Kyle and his brothers had played it so much when they were younger, Mrs. Keeley wrote to Mr. Lemoncello's company for a refresher pack of clue cards. The new cards listed all sorts of different bizarro stuff you needed to find, like "an adult's droopy underpants," "one dirty dish," and "a rotten banana peel."

(At the end of the game, the losers had to put everything back exactly where the items had been found. It was an official rule, printed inside the top of the box, and made winning the game that much more important!)

While Curtis was stranded next door, trying to talk the neighbor's Doberman, Twinky, out of his favorite tug toy, Kyle and Mike were both searching for the same two items, because for the final round, all the players were given the same Riddle Card.

That day's riddle, even though it was a card Kyle had never seen before, had been extra easy.

FIND TWO COINS FROM 1982 THAT ADD UP TO THIRTY CENTS AND ONE OF THEM CANNOT BE A NICKEL.

Duh. The answer was a quarter and a nickel because the riddle said only *one* of them couldn't be a nickel.

So to win, Kyle had to find a 1982 quarter *and* a 1982 nickel.

Also easy.

Their dad kept an apple cider jug filled with loose change down in his basement workshop.

That's why Kyle and Mike were racing to get there first.

Mike bolted through the front door.

Kyle grinned.

He loved playing games against his big brothers. As the youngest, it was just about the only chance he ever got to beat them fair and square. Board games leveled the playing field. You needed a good roll of the dice, a lucky draw of the cards, and some smarts, but if things went your way and you gave it your all, anyone could win.

Especially today, since Mike had blown his lead by choosing the standard route down to the basement. He'd go through the front door, tear to the back of the house, bound down the steps, and then run to their dad's workshop.

Kyle, on the other hand, would take a shortcut.

He hopped over a couple of boxy shrubs and kicked open the low-to-the-ground casement window. He heard something crackle when his tennis shoe hit the windowpane, but he couldn't worry about it. He had to beat his big brother.

He crawled through the narrow opening, dropped to the floor, and scrabbled over to the workbench, where he found the jug, dumped out the coins, and started sifting through the sea of pennies, nickels, dimes, and quarters.

Score!

Kyle quickly uncovered a 1982 nickel. He tucked it into his shirt pocket and sent pennies, nickels, and dimes skidding across the floor as he concentrated on quarters. 2010. 2003. 1986.

"Come on, come on," he muttered.

The workshop door swung open.

"What the . . . ?" Mike was surprised to see that Kyle had beaten him to the coin jar.

Mike fell to his knees and started searching for his own

coins just as Kyle shouted, "Got it!" and plucked a 1982 quarter out of the pile.

"What about the nickel?" demanded Mike.

Kyle pulled it out of his shirt pocket.

"You went through the window?" said a voice from outside.

It was Curtis. Kneeling in the flower beds.

"Yeah," said Kyle.

"I was going to do that. The shortest distance between two points is a straight line."

"I can't believe you won!" moaned Mike, who wasn't used to losing *anything*.

"Well," said Kyle, standing up and strutting a little, "believe it, brother. Because now you two *losers* have to put all the junk back."

"I am *not* taking this back to Twinky!" said Curtis. He held up a very slimy, knotted rope.

"Oh, yes you are," said Kyle. "Because you *lost*. Oh sure, you *thought* about using the window. . . ."

"Um, Kyle?" mumbled Curtis. "You might want to shut up. . . ."

"What? C'mon, Curtis. Don't be such a sore loser. Just because I was the one who took the shortcut and kicked open the window and—"

"You did this, Kyle?"

A new face appeared in the window.

Their dad's.

"Heh, heh, heh," chuckled Mike behind Kyle.

"You broke the glass?" Their father sounded ticked off. "Well, guess who's going to pay to have this window replaced."

That's why Kyle Keeley had fifty cents deducted from his allowance for the rest of the year.

And got grounded for a week.

2

Halfway across town, Dr. Yanina Zinchenko, the world-
famous librarian, was walking briskly through the cavern-
ous building that was only days away from its gala grand
opening.

Alexandriaville's new public library had been under
construction for five years. All work had been done with
the utmost secrecy under the tightest possible security. One
crew did the exterior renovations on what had once been
the small Ohio city's most magnificent building, the Gold
Leaf Bank. Other crews—carpenters, masons, electricians,
and plumbers—worked on the interior.

No single construction crew stayed on the job longer
than six weeks.

No crew knew what any of the other crews had done
(or would be doing).

And when all those crews were finished, several

super-secret covert crews (highly paid workers who would deny ever having been near the library, Alexandriaville, *or* the state of Ohio) stealthily applied the final touches.

Dr. Zinchenko had supervised the construction project for her employer—a very eccentric (some would say loony) billionaire. Only she knew all the marvels and wonders the incredible new library would hold (and hide) within its walls.

Dr. Zinchenko was a tall woman with blazing-red hair. She wore an expensive, custom-tailored business suit, jazzy high-heeled shoes, a Bluetooth earpiece, and glasses with thick red frames.

Heels clicking on the marble floor, fingers tapping on the glass of her very advanced tablet computer, Dr. Zinchenko strode past the control center's red door, under an arch, and into the breathtakingly large circular reading room beneath the library's three-story-tall rotunda.

The bank building, which provided the shell for the new library, had been built in 1931. With towering Corinthian columns, an arched entryway, lots of fancy trim, and a mammoth shimmering gold dome, the building looked like it belonged next door to the triumphant memorials in Washington, D.C.—not on this small Ohio town's quaint streets.

Dr. Zinchenko paused to stare up at the library's most stunning visual effect: the Wonder Dome. Ten wedge-shaped, high-definition video screens—as brilliant as those in Times Square—lined the underbelly of the dome like so many orange slices. Each screen could operate independently or as part of a spectacular whole. The Wonder Dome could become the constellations of the night sky; a flight through the clouds that made viewers below sense that the whole building had somehow lifted off the ground; or, in Dewey decimal mode, ten sections depicting vibrant and constantly changing images associated with each category in the library cataloging system.

"I have the final numbers for the fourth sector of the Wonder Dome in Dewey mode," Dr. Zinchenko said into her Bluetooth earpiece. "364 point 1092." She carefully over-enunciated each word to make certain the video artist knew what specific numbers should occasionally drift across the fourth wedge amid the swirling social-sciences montage featuring a floating judge's gavel, a tumbling teacher's apple, and a gentle snowfall of holiday icons. "The numbers, however, should not appear until eleven a.m. Sunday. Is that clear?"

"Yes, Dr. Zinchenko," replied the tinny voice in her ear.

Next Dr. Zinchenko studied the holographic statues projected into black crepe-lined recesses cut into the massive stone piers that supported the arched windows from which the Wonder Dome rose.

"Why are Shakespeare and Dickens still here? They're not on the list for opening night."

"Sorry," replied the library's director of holographic imagery, who was also on the conference call. "I'll fix it."

"Thank you."

Exiting the rotunda, the librarian entered the Children's Room.

It was dim, with only a few work lights glowing, but Dr. Zinchenko had memorized the layout of the miniature tables and was able to march, without bumping her shins, to the Story Corner for a final check on her recently installed geese.

The flock of six audio-animatronic goslings—fluffy robots with ping-pongish eyeballs (created for the new library by imagineers who used to work at Disney World)—stood perched atop an angled bookcase in the corner. Mother Goose, in her bonnet and granny glasses, was frozen in the center.

"This is librarian One," said Dr. Zinchenko, loud enough for the microphones hidden in the ceiling to pick up her voice. "Initiate story-time sequence."

The geese sprang to mechanical life.

"Nursery rhyme."

The geese honked out "Baa-Baa Black Sheep" in six-part harmony.

"Treasure Island?"

The birds yo-ho-ho'ed their way through "Fifteen Men on a Dead Man's Chest."

Dr. Zinchenko clapped her hands. The rollicking geese stopped singing and swaying.

"One more," she said. Squinting, she saw a book sitting on a nearby table. *"Walter the Farting Dog."*

The six geese spun around and farted, their tail feathers flipping up in sync with the noisy blasts.

"Excellent. End story time."

The geese slumped back into their sleep mode. Dr. Zinchenko made one more tick on her computer tablet. Her final punch list was growing shorter and shorter, which was a very good thing. The library's grand opening was set for Friday night. Dr. Z and her army of associates had only a few days left to smooth out any kinks in the library's complex operating system.

Suddenly, Dr. Zinchenko heard a low, rumbling growl.

Turning around, she was eyeball to icy-blue eyeball with a very rare white tiger.

Dr. Zinchenko sighed and touched her Bluetooth earpiece.

"Ms. G? This is Dr. Z. What is our white Bengal tiger doing in the children's department? . . . I see. Apparently, there was a slight misunderstanding. We do not want him permanently positioned near *The Jungle Book*. Check the call number. 599 point 757. . . . Right. He should be in Zoology. . . . Yes, please. Right away. Thank you, Ms. G."

And like a vanishing mirage, the tiger disappeared.

WHAT IF YOU COULD LEARN EVERYTHING JUST BY EATING JELLY BEANS?

Meet the Smartest Kid in the Universe and find out in this fun-packed new series by Chris Grabenstein!

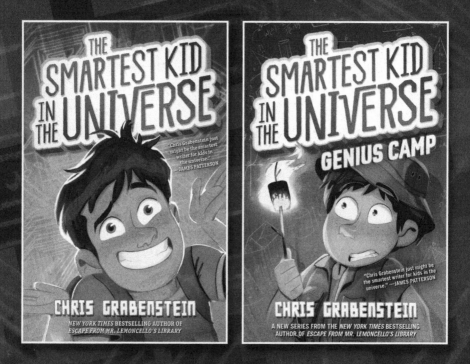

J.J. Grabenstein

CHRIS GRABENSTEIN

is the *New York Times* bestselling author of the hilarious and award-winning Mr. Lemoncello's Library, Welcome to Wonderland, and Smartest Kid in the Universe series, *The Island of Dr. Libris, Shine!* (coauthored with J.J. Grabenstein), *Dog Squad,* and many other books, as well as the coauthor of numerous page-turners with James Patterson, including *Best Nerds Forever,* and the Jackie Ha-Ha, Treasure Hunters, and Max Einstein series. Chris lives in New York City with his wife, J.J.

CHRISGRABENSTEIN.COM